HIT AND DRAG

HIT AND DRAG

A Ham Marks, MD, Medical Murder Mystery

WILLIAM H. SIMON, MD

HIT AND DRAG
A Ham Marks, MD, Medical Murder Mystery

iUniverse books may be ordered through booksellers or by contacting:

iUniverse
1663 Liberty Drive
Bloomington, IN 47403
www.iuniverse.com
1-800-Authors (1-800-288-4677)

Because of the dynamic nature of the Internet, any web addresses or links contained in this book may have changed since publication and may no longer be valid. The views expressed in this work are solely those of the author and do not necessarily reflect the views of the publisher, and the publisher hereby disclaims any responsibility for them.

Any people depicted in stock imagery provided by Thinkstock are models, and such images are being used for illustrative purposes only. Certain stock imagery © Thinkstock.

ISBN: 978-1-4917-6393-3 (sc)
ISBN: 978-1-4917-6394-0 (hc)
ISBN: 978-1-4917-6392-6 (e)

Library of Congress Control Number: 2015905902

Print information available on the last page.

iUniverse rev. date: 05/05/2015

I wish to dedicate this book to my loving wife, Michele Simon. I also want to acknowledge her help and criticism as she stood by me for the length of time that it has taken me to write this book. She also worries about me a lot when I'm out playing golf.

TABLE OF CONTENTS

Chapter 1 - The End of the Beginning, the Beginning 1
Chapter 2 - The beginning—really! 11
Chapter 3 - All Is Not Quiet on the Front Nine 19
Chapter 4 - Rasher's Swan Song 26
Chapter 5 - Dead Men Tell No Lies 32
Chapter 6 - Water, Water, Everywhere, but Don't Drink It! 37
Chapter 7 - No Good Deed Goes Unpunished............................42
Chapter 8 - Serious, but Not Fatal....................................48
Chapter 9 - The Blame Game...51
Chapter 10 - The Water Doctor 59
Chapter 11 - Return to Zion 64
Chapter 12 - When Is a Farmhouse Not a Farmhouse?...................70
Chapter 13 - Frack, Baby, Frack! 74
Chapter 14 - A Summer Shower Brings No Flowers.....................79
Chapter 15 - Justice Was Not Blind That Day 83
Chapter 16 - All's Quiet on the Southern Course 87
Chapter 17 - The Court Speaks 97
Chapter 18 - The Golf Widow 100
Chapter 19 - Is a Murderer Still Out There? 107
Chapter 20 - Vinnie and the Vig......................................109
Chapter 21 - Setting the Bait...110
Chapter 22 - The Shark's Lair 114
Chapter 23 - Who Did It, or Didn't Do It? 118
Chapter 24 - Marshal Marks 123

Chapter One

THE END OF THE BEGINNING, THE BEGINNING ...

Rules of the modern-day game of golf were established by the Society of St. Andrews in Scotland around 1754. Today the rules are maintained by the Royal and Ancient Golf Club of St. Andrews (the R&A, based in St. Andrews, Scotland) in Great Britain and Europe, and the United Stated Golf Association (USGA, based in Far Hills, New Jersey) in the USA and Mexico.

It was quiet—incredibly quiet. No wind was blowing through the trees. No birdsong. An occasional insect buzzed by.

Three men stood like statues on the perfectly manicured grass surface of the eighteenth green of the south course of the Split Rock Golf Club in Horsham, Pennsylvania. All three men wore shorts on this warm Wednesday in June of 2014. They each wore a collared sports shirt, as per club regulations; a baseball-type hat, with the logo of the Split Rock Golf Club on it (a split rock with three golf clubs growing out of it in a fan shape); and spiked shoes (either brown-and-white or all white).

Ben Fowler, fifty-five, a lawyer from Bluebell, Pennsylvania, was bent like a pretzel over a small white golf ball that lay four feet from the hole in the perfect green surface. He was making short practice strokes with a short club that had a flat blade at its end (a putter).

Standing five feet away from Ben, out of his shadow and line of sight, was sixty-four-year-old Albert Ducasian, a farmer from Bucks County who had retired from farming after he had licensed the oil rights to his five hundred acres of land to Recovery Oil Company. The oil company was paying Ducasian $40,000 per month for the oil rights to his land and would pay him much more if oil or gas were actually pumped out of his land by a process called hydraulic fracturing, or fracking. Ducasian was steadying himself against the grass surface with a long pole topped by a small yellow flag bearing the number eighteen and, again, the Split Rock logo.

The third man was large—six feet two inches, weighing about 230 pounds. His name was Ham Marks—Dr. Ham Marks, from Wayne, Pennsylvania. He was an orthopedic surgeon who had given up his surgical practice for a medical legal forensic practice, one in which it was his job to determine the cause of a musculoskeletal problem—be it a natural cause or an accidental or work-related cause. He also stood out of the line of sight of Ben Fowler, leaning against his putter as it rested on the manicured green surface.

Both Ham and Ducasian had already putted out. They had rolled their golf balls into the plastic-coated hole and were holding their golf balls in their hands, waiting for Ben to finish so they could all get back in their electric golf carts and return to the club's golf pro shop on this particularly beautiful summer day.

The two golf carts were parked, one in front of the other, on an asphalt pathway about twenty feet from the eighteenth green.

In the second cart sat the fourth player in the group. He was not dressed like the others. He wore neither hat nor shirt. His trunk was covered by a large green towel (with the logo of the Split Rock Golf Club on it). Another green towel was wrapped around his waist, and his bare feet were wrapped in a third towel. This was sixty-two-year-old Martin Rasher. Rasher was originally from northern New Jersey, but now he lived in Horsham. He owned fifteen Delicious Donut Shoppes in New Jersey and spent his time, when he wasn't playing golf, riding in his Cadillac from one store to the next, picking up money from the franchisee and checking the income statements for each store.

He had suffered an accidental fall into a pond at the tenth tee and had been in the cart, wrapped in towels, since then.

At this point, as Ben Fowler practiced for what he hoped to be his final putt, Rasher croaked out what sounded to all like "Hi, Ben! Hi, Ben!"

Ben, who was used to this man's disrupting the play of himself and his co-players throughout the eighteen holes, stopped his swing, picked up his head, and stared at Rasher. He then shook his head from side to side and returned to his pretzel-like stance over the ball.

Within seconds, Rasher croaked again. "Hi, happy Ben! Hi, happy Ben!"

This time Ben picked his club up, laid it on his shoulder, stared at Martin Rasher, and shouted, "For God's sake, will you please shut up, Martin!"

Then he looked embarrassedly at the other two players and said, "I'm sorry, guys, but I'm putting, for God's sake," knowing that he had broken one of the rules of golf etiquette by shouting, even though he had been provoked by Rasher.

Ben placed his putter on the green, took two quick practice strokes, and struck the ball lightly. The ball rolled forward, took a slight turn from right to left, and fell into the hole with a *clickety-clack* sound.

"Nice putt," said Al Ducasian, returning the flag into the cup.

Ham put out his hand to both Al and Ben and said, "Nice round. Thanks, guys."

"Well, if nothing else, it was the weirdest round of golf I've ever played," said Fowler as he and Ducasian mounted their cart and drove off to the clubhouse. They each punched the number of strokes it had taken them to complete the eighteenth hole into the computer screen mounted in the cart. The screen totaled their scores individually for the round and automatically sent the data to the pro shop, where the score was collected in the computer's memory in order to calculate their handicaps automatically on a quarterly basis.

Ham Marks turned, his putter in one hand and his golf ball in the other, and began to approach his golf cart. He suddenly changed direction as he spotted, with his peripheral vision, his wife approaching the eighteenth green from the clubhouse.

"Hi, dear," Ham said. "What have you been doing?" His wife, Ruth, herself a both a private-practice pediatrician and a research physician at Bryn Mawr Hospital, gave Ham a big hug and a kiss. She didn't have to stand on her tiptoes to reach Ham's cheek, since she stood at five feet ten inches in her sneakers. Her body was slim and well honed by biweekly workouts.

"I was playing mah-jongg," Ruth said. "You remember I learned the game on the cruise we took."

"Oh yes," Ham answered. "Well, good for you."

"Ham, I was watching you on the eighteenth green from the clubhouse. It seemed to me that there were only three of you. Didn't you start with a foursome?" Ruth queried.

"I did, dear," Ham answered. "But it has been a very unusual golf game today. One of the men, Marty Rasher—you know, the man who owns those fifteen Delicious Donut Shoppes—was injured on the tenth hole, and he rode in the cart for the rest of the game. Come on over with me, and take a look at him. He fell in the tee-side pond, and I had to rescue him. He was nauseated and shocky, and I had to start CPR because I thought he had swallowed a lot of the pond water—which incidentally smelled awful. He came around quickly, so I didn't call for an ambulance right away, but I told the golf pro via ARNI to have Abington Hospital on standby in case we needed to send him over there. He is sitting in my golf cart, and I think he's all right. He certainly was enough of a pain in the butt while we were putting on the eighteenth— hollering out at Ben Fowler. Come on, let's go take a look at him."

With that, Ham and Ruth approached Ham's parked golf cart and saw Marty Rasher slumped in the passenger's seat, somewhat disheveled and half-naked, his shirt and shoes in a damp pile next to him.

Ham placed his hand on Rasher's shoulder and said, "Marty, Marty! Are you okay?" Thinking that the man might have fallen asleep, Ham shook him gently and said in a louder voice, "Marty, Marty, wake up!"

With a final shake of the slumped man's shoulder, Ham stepped back as Martin Rasher—all five feet seven inches and two hundred pounds of him—fell out of the cart and onto his side on the ground.

Ruth bent over the fallen man as Ham rolled him on his back, keeping his head turned to prevent aspiration if he should begin to vomit.

"Ham, he's not breathing!" Ruth said. She pressed her fingers to his neck as she tilted his head back. "And I can't feel a pulse in his neck."

"Well, start CPR on his chest while I notify emergency services; I can take over after that," Ham said, knowing his wife had passed her required CPR course several times.

Ruth straddled Rasher's supine body, placed her hand over his substernal area in the middle of his chest, crossed her opposite palm over the first, and started forceful, quick downward thrusts, counting, "one one-thousand, two one-thousand ..." as she did so.

Ham reached into the cart and pressed a red button.

"Hello, Dr. Marks, how may I help you?" a robotic male voice asked.

"ARNI, call the pro shop—emergency!" Ham said, using as a name the initialism for "automatic reporting numerical identifier."

"Right away, Dr. Marks," the machine voice answered, and suddenly a loud, rapid ringing was heard through the cart's built-in speaker. Almost immediately a voice answered and said, "Pro shop, John speaking. How may I help you?"

"John!" Ham shouted (although he didn't have to—ARNI's microphone was very sensitive). "We've got an emergency! Marty Rasher has had an accident, and he suddenly stopped breathing. I asked you to have Abington Hospital Emergency Services on call. Please call them and have them come out here immediately, with the police. We are here at the eighteenth green."

"I know where you are, Dr. Marks. Emergency services will be with you in about five minutes."

"Thanks, John." Ham turned to Ruth. "EMTs will be here in a few minutes. Let me take over CPR."

Ham waited until Ruth gave a thrust to Rasher's thoracic cage and diaphragm and quickly moved away. Ham then assumed the same position she had occupied, and began the timed thrusts.

"You know, Ham, the latest research says that one should keep up CPR longer than previously thought before giving up."

"Yes, dear, I read the article," Ham said between thrusts.

When the ambulance arrived a few minutes later, Ham was still applying CPR. A small crowd had gathered, including the two golf pros, the parking valet, and two members of the grounds crew.

The EMTs ran from the ambulance. One replaced Ham, giving CPR. The other applied an oxygen mask to Rasher's face over a short plastic endotracheal mouthpiece, as well as an automatic pulse-and-blood-pressure recorder to his left arm. Then, brandishing two defibrillator paddles, he called "Clear!" At that point the other EMT stopped the CPR maneuver and leaned back, with his knees on the ground on either side of Rasher's legs. The EMT with the paddles applied them to Rasher's chest while a third helper punched the red button on the defibrillator. Rasher's upper body jumped with the defibrillator shock and then settled back on the grass.

"No pulse, no BP or respiration," the third assistant cried out, at which point the EMT with the paddles cried "Clear!" again and repeated the shocking procedure.

"Still no pulse or BP," the assistant stated firmly.

The second EMT resumed his straddling position and began CPR once again.

"How long has he been without a pulse or respiration?" the EMT with the shock paddles asked Ham.

"Well I'd say about twenty minutes—wouldn't you, Ruth?"

Ruth just nodded in the affirmative.

"Okay, we'll give him two more shocks and then call it all over. Clear!"

Two more shocks were given, and the assistant with the machinery said, "Still no pulse, BP, or respiration."

"Okay. It's all over. Everybody agree?" the EMT said, pulling down the paddles and turning off the defibrillator. The other two men nodded and moved away from the body.

"We'll take him to the Abington ER and have the doc there officially declare him dead. Does anyone here want to ride with us?"

No one spoke until Ham said, "I'll call his wife. I'm sure she'll want to see him in the ER."

"Thanks. What is your name, in case anyone in the ER has any questions?"

"I'm Dr. Ham Marks, an orthopedic surgeon. My cell number is 864-706-4113."

"Well thanks, Doc, for giving it a try," the EMT said as he recorded Ham's information, noted the time on his wristwatch, and recorded that on his clipboard as well.

"I have that his name was Martin Rasher and he was sixty-two years old, right?"

"Right," said Ham. "I really don't know any of his medical history."

"That's all right, Doc; we'll get the rest from his wife."

The two EMTs moved Rasher onto a stretcher, covered him— including his face—with a sheet, and transported him to the ambulance.

The remaining crowd stared ahead in silence as the ambulance drove off.

Ruth turned to Ham and said, "That was perfectly awful, Ham. What happened out on the golf course?"

"I'll tell you later, dear. Right now I'd better get his wife's telephone number and call her. She wasn't playing mah-jongg with you, was she?"

"No, Ham, I played with three other women."

"Well now, let's try ARNI for Mrs. Rasher's phone number."

With that, Ham pushed the red button on the golf cart again and heard "Yes, Dr. Marks. How can I help you?"

"ARNI," Ham said, having been trained how to interact with the robotic computer system shortly after joining the club, "can you give me the cell phone number for Mrs. Martin Rasher?"

"Yes, of course, Dr. Marks. Are you ready to record it?"

"Yes," Ham said, holding his scorecard and a pencil. "Go ahead."

"Here it is: 864-633-0774. Got that?" ARNI stated.

"Yes, thank you, ARNI."

"You are welcome, Dr. Marks. Is Mr. Martin Rasher okay? He seems to have disappeared from my system."

"No, ARNI, I'm afraid Mr. Rasher is gone from your system permanently."

"I'm sorry to hear that, Dr. Marks. Good-bye, and have a nice day."

Ham did not reply further but dialed the phone number given to him by ARNI on his own cell phone. The phone rang. On the third ring, someone picked up the phone and a female voice with a Jersey accent, somewhat rough and alto, said, "Hello. Who is this?"

"Mrs. Rasher, this is Dr. Ham Marks."

"Yeah? Who're you, and why you callin'?"

"Mrs. Rasher, I played golf with your husband Marty today, and he had an accident."

"Yeah? He shoulda had two accidents—leavin' me for that lousy golf game every weekend."

"Well, this accident caused severe shock, and I'm afraid he didn't make it."

"Didn't make it? Whatcha talkin' about?"

"I'm afraid that despite all attempts to revive him by emergency medical people, he passed away."

There was silence on the other end of Ham's cell phone. Ham spoke again. "He was taken to Abington Hospital Emergency Room. You can see him there."

"See 'im dead? Is that whatcha mean?"

"Yes, I'm afraid so, Mrs. Rasher. I'll give you my cell phone number, and you can call me if you have any questions. I'll try to answer them." Ham then gave her his cell phone number.

"Okay, thanks. I'll call from the ER."

"Fine. I'm awfully sorry, Mrs. Rasher."

"Okay, thanks." She hung up.

"By the way, Ham, did you notice the severe periorbital edema around Martin Rasher's eyes?"

"No, Ruth dear, I was concentrating on finding a pulse or some sign of respiration."

"Well, I've seen similar signs in some of my severely allergic children," Ruth, the pediatrician, observed.

"There certainly were enough allergens in that smelly water that he accidently swallowed," Ham explained.

As Ham clicked the off button on his phone, a deep male voice said, "Dr. Marks, can I speak to you for a minute?"

Ham turned and found a six-foot-tall uniformed police officer standing next to him. His gray hair was cropped short, and he wore a sergeant's stripes on his sleeves. He held his cap under one arm, and a pen and notebook in his hands.

"Of course, Officer. What would you like to know?"

"Well first of all, doctor, I want you to know that I'm just getting preliminary information. A county detective will follow up and collect all the details, okay?"

"Sure thing, Officer, you can contact me at any time," Ham offered.

"Fine, thank you. Now, can you briefly tell me what happened to Martin Rasher?" the officer continued.

Ham spotted a nametag on the officer's chest reading "McGuire." He looked up at the man and said, "Sure, Officer McGuire, here's a short story of what happened. On the tenth tee—excuse me, do you know anything about golf, Officer?"

"Sure," McGuire said.

"Okay, on the tenth tee, Marty Rasher fell into a pond. He swallowed some water—which by the way smelled awful—and he couldn't get out, even though the pond was only two feet deep. I went in to drag him out. Then I had to perform CPR for a few minutes. He coughed up water and came around. Afterward he was nauseated, so we put him in my cart, wrapped him in towels, and contacted the pro shop to notify

Abington Hospital to meet us with an ambulance when we came in. We were playing golf in a foursome: me, Martin, Albert Ducasian, and Ben Fowler."

Officer McGuire said, "Hold it, Doc, let me get those names down … Okay. So you didn't call 911 at that point?"

"No. Marty said he didn't want emergency care at that point. In fact, he was talking like his old disrupting self. He even shouted out to us when we were putting on the eighteenth green."

"So he was still alive up until a few minutes before you reached him; is that right?" the officer queried.

"Yes, Officer. My wife, who is also a physician—a pediatrician—and I got to Marty about five minutes after he last spoke."

"And he was dead?"

"Well, he had no pulse or respiration, and we couldn't revive him with CPR for about ten minutes. Then the emergency medical crew arrived," Ham replied.

"What caused his death?"

"I don't know, Officer; perhaps an autopsy will reveal the cause. I just know that he swallowed some of the foul-smelling pond water," Ham answered.

"Well, I'll send a member of our police lab out to take a sample of the water. Anything else you can think of?" the officer said, still holding his pencil and the pad on which he was recording Ham's answers.

"My wife noted that he had periorbital edema—swelling around the eyes—which is often a sign of severe allergic reaction," Ham added.

"Well thanks, Doc. I'm sure the detective assigned to this case will have more questions for you and the other two members of your foursome. Can you give me a telephone number where he can reach you?"

"Sure, Officer, my cell phone number is 864-706-4113," Ham offered.

"Thanks, Doc. I'm going to the Abington Hospital ER now. If you think of anything else that is helpful, just give me a ring," the officer said as he gave Ham a card with his name and number on it.

The officer returned to his car and left the club, speaking on the radio clipped to his shoulder as he departed.

Ham turned to his wife and said, "I'd better find Ben and Al in the locker room and explain what happened, and that the police will be contacting them. Then I'll shower and change and meet you at the valet station."

"Okay, Ham," Ruth said, still shaking her head in disbelief. Ham kissed Ruth on the cheek, and they both hurried off in different directions.

Chapter Two

THE BEGINNING—REALLY!

Early golf courses were known as "links" courses. They were placed on coastal land, mainly in Scotland.

Presently, there are between 15,000 and 20,000 golf courses in the United States. Each course occupies between 110 and 190 acres. 29% of the land is dedicated to fairway (short grass), while 60% is used as "rough" (long grass). The rest of the acreage is taken up by the greens (very short grass), tee boxes, sand traps (bunkers), water hazards (streams, ponds, lakes), and other hazards or out-of-bounds areas (trees and bushes, golf paths, etc.).

The length of a standard golf course is between 5,000 and 7,000 yards. The length varies according to the tee box, the farthest point from the green that the player starts from on each hole. Each tee box is marked by colored markers: black or gold for scratch (zero handicapped players), blue for low-handicapped men, white for senior men, and red for ladies or handicapped men.

Each course is divided into 18 holes: 9 in the "front 9," and 9 in the "back 9."

Each 9 requires between 32 and 36 strokes of the ball (par) by a scratch player (a player with a zero handicap). Each hole varies between requiring 3, 4, or 5 strokes. If a player reaches the cup on a hole in the established number of strokes, he (or she) has made par. If one under par, he or she has made a birdie. If two strokes under par, the player has made an eagle, and if three under (very rare), an albatross (or double eagle).

One stroke over par is known as a bogey, two over a double-bogey, three over a triple bogey, and so forth.

The object of the game is for one player to reach the 18th cup (on the 18th green) using the lowest number of strokes.

Ham Marks, MD, drove his silver 500 SEL Mercedes with the sunroof open on the Pennsylvania Turnpike. He was traveling from his home in Wayne, Pennsylvania, to his club, Split Rock Golf Club, in Horsham, Pennsylvania. Ham was not his first name. His mother, a classicist, had given him the name Homer Alcibiades Marks. This mouthful got shortened to HAM, or Ham Marks, a long time back in his sixty-four years on Earth.

He had worked hard as an orthopedic surgeon for over thirty years and had made a good living for his wife and family. In the last few years, arthritis in his hands and spine had made it virtually impossible for him to spend many hours at any one time in the operating room. So he had become a nonoperating orthopedic surgeon, specializing in musculoskeletal forensics.

He had played golf as a teenager but gave it up when he went to medical school. With his increased freedom from time devoted to emergency care and the long hours involved in the operating room and carrying out postoperative hospital care, he had taken up the sport again. The one compensation he had made for his age and his arthritis was to use extra-thick wrapping on the grips of his golf clubs to make it easier for him to grasp them.

The golf club he had chosen to join, Split Rock Golf Club, was relatively new (three years old). It was situated in Horsham, Pennsylvania, forty-three minutes away by car from his home in Wayne.

There were several reasons why he had chosen this club over the dozens of better-known clubs in the area. First, it was new. The two eighteen-hole courses, North Course and South Course, had been designed by the famous Golden Bear Corporation and were magnificently landscaped. The north course was slightly longer and more difficult than the south course. Ham stuck with the south course, except when he really wanted to embarrass himself.

The club was wife and family friendly. It had an Olympic-sized swimming pool, six clay tennis courts, and a fully equipped spa and workout area with whirlpool baths and steam baths. His wife, Ruth

Marks, MD, loved this aspect of the club life and used the facilities once or twice each week.

There was a sports bar with six large flat-screen TVs. A grill room was available for lunch and light meals, and a three-star restaurant served lunch and dinner.

The club chef, Frank Basker, was Cordon Bleu trained and had been the chief chef at a well-known French restaurant in downtown Philadelphia.

For all this luxury, the costs were relatively low. An entrance bond (to be paid back on withdrawal from the club—after ten years of membership), was $50,000, to be paid over three years. The annual golf fees (there were no non-golf members) were $10,000 with additional greens fees and cart fees. There were occasional assessments, but every club had these.

The most enticing reason for Ham to join this particular club was the advanced technology Split Rock had incorporated into every aspect of club life. Every new member had to spend at least three hours learning the use of the club card. The club card was just slightly thicker than a charge card and could be carried in a man's or woman's wallet. It incorporated Bluetooth technology, GPS technology, and a computer system that used ARNI as an interface.

As Ham exited the Pennsylvania Turnpike and drove onto the CDP (census-designated place) of Horsham, Pennsylvania, he marveled at the orderliness and beauty of the flowers and trees lining the streets. Horsham had been voted the fifteenth best place to live in the USA in a 2007 issue of *Money* magazine. It boasted a population of over 15,000 souls with a mediian income over $85,000 and a median age of 37.5.

Ham turned left off of Easton Road and onto Horsham Drive. In one mile he came to Tournament Road and made a right turn. He had to slow down at the unmanned gates of the Split Rock Country Club. The ten-foot-high wrought-iron gates, topped by the club logo and the name of the Split Rock Golf Club, began to open in a matter of seconds. As Ham drove through the gates, he heard a familiar male voice: "Good morning, Dr. Marks. It is 8:30 a.m. on Wednesday, June 12. How are you today?"

"I'm just fine, ARNI," Ham said, not giving a thought to the fact that he was talking to a computer.

"I have arranged a 9:00 a.m. tee time on the south course with three men in your handicap range" (Ham had a twenty-five handicap—more about that later).

Since Ham was a relatively new member of the club, he didn't have a regular golf game with longtime friends who were club members, so he relied on the computer to set up a foursome for him. As long as he wasn't particularly finicky about his playing companions, this was a good system for him. He got to know the men at the club with similar golf talents and it was simply easier to rely on ARNI than to round up three other men to play at a particular day and time.

There was one kicker. Once ARNI had established the four players for the game, no one player (who didn't call in from a hospital bed or a jail cell) could opt out of the foursome without a considerable penalty. The penalty was that ARNI would not allow the offending member to play on either course again on that particular day until everyone who wanted to play had had his turn—usually by about 5:00 or 6:00 p.m. that day. So you took what you got, no matter the reputation of or gossip about any player.

"Dr. Marks, today you will play with Mr. Ben Fowler, Mr. Albert Ducasian, and Mr. Martin Rasher. Is that satisfactory for you?"

"Yes, ARNI. That's just fine," Ham said, knowing that a negative response to the computer selection would result in a bad day at Split Rock.

"Thank you, Dr. Marks. Have a good day," ARNI responded.

Ham drove slowly (minding the ten-mile-per-hour speed limit) up to the large, rambling sandstone clubhouse, passing the magnificently groomed golf course on either side of the road. The clubhouse architecture reminded Ham of an old Philadelphia Main Line mansion. As he approached the club's front door and the awaiting valet, he thought about his partners for the day.

He didn't know any one of them well, so he considered their reputations as according to locker-room gossip.

Ben Fowler was a general lawyer with an office in nearby Bluebell. The gossip was that he had done very well over the years, mainly dealing with farmers and local businessmen. In fact, he was the lawyer for Martin Rasher and had helped him obtain his multiple Delicious Donut franchises. There was some rumble about the locker room that there was a bit of bad blood between Fowler and Rasher over some fees that the "baker" owed the lawyer.

Albert Ducasian was an old-time Bucks County farmer, plain as an ear of corn. It certainly wasn't his fault (or his genius) that had led to the fortune he was reaping from leasing the oil and mineral rights to his farm to a rich oil company. He was happy that he no longer had to milk cows and crank up the tractor at 5:00 a.m., but he had expressed concerns to his locker roommates that he hoped the fracking wasn't poisoning his well water.

Martin Rasher, the donut king, was another story. He had a bad rep. He was known to be loud, obnoxious, and a golf cheater. Ham, in his many years practicing orthopedic surgery, had run into patients with similar defects, and he felt that he could handle the situation.

Ham drove his car under the club's porte cochere and up to the valet parking area, where a young valet named Joe, dressed in dark shorts and a white shirt with epaulettes, was waiting to open his driver's-side door and park his car.

On the opposite side of the car was the natural symbol for which the club was named—a large granite bolder, about four feet high and six feet wide, with a crevice down its middle. Growing from this crevice were large sunflowers, not golf clubs. But all in all, the rock made for a fitting symbol and logo for the Split Rock Golf Club.

The valet opened the driver's door and said, "Good morning, Dr. Marks. All set for a day of golf?"

"I sure am, Joe," answered Ham as he noted an erythematous vesicular rash on Joe's left forearm.

"What's with the rash, Joe?"

"Oh, I must have brushed against something growing on the golf course when I parked one of the cars. I'm really sensitive to poison ivy and stuff," Joe answered as he exchanged places with Ham in the Mercedes driver seat.

"I hope you've seen a doctor about it. That's a wicked-looking rash," Ham said sympathetically.

"Oh yes, he gave me some steroid cream to put on it," Joe said.

"Well, that's good," Ham said as he waved Joe and his car off to its parking spot.

The car had been tagged by the club card and would be parked in a spot assigned by the computer. The spot would register on a screen at the valet desk so that the valet could inform an inquisitive member as to who was at the club at any time of the day or night.

Ham had been concerned about the valet's rash, so he had forgotten to ask if his playing partners were already there, but he would find out soon enough when he entered the locker room.

Ham walked through the tiled lobby with its six-foot bouquet of beautiful flowers on a center table. He turned right and passed through the grill room and sports bar as he headed toward the men's locker room. The head chef, Frank Basker, was clearing some breakfast dishes and setting up coffee and morning and afternoon snacks in his toque and white chef's uniform. Ham noted that he looked very down in the mouth—an unusual visage for the usually jovial chef.

"Why so gloomy, Chef?" Ham asked.

The chef looked up and smiled at Ham and said, "I'm sorry for the sad look, Dr. Marks, but Tom died."

"I'm so sorry, chef, who's Tom?" asked Ham sympathetically.

"Oh, I'm talking about Tom, the housecat," said the chef with a bit of a sad chuckle. "I came into the kitchen at six this morning, and there he was, lying out on the floor dead."

"What did he die of?" Ham asked.

"I have no idea. He's ordinarily a very healthy cat. He goes out at night and catches field mice on the golf course, but I have no idea why he died."

"Well, I'm sorry, Chef. He obviously meant something to you."

"Thanks, Dr. Marks. He was a nice cat, and I'll miss him," said the chef as he waved to Ham on his way back to the kitchen.

Ham continued on to the locker room and waved hello to the locker room attendant. "Hi, Charlie."

"Hi, Dr. Marks. Your playing partners have already been here. They're out on the putting green warming up for you."

"Thanks, Charlie," Ham said as he opened his locker door. The door had unlocked automatically as Ham approached, and it would lock when he departed—under the control of Ham's club card. Each locker door had a numerical pad that could also be used to open the door if the member somehow got separated temporarily from his club card, or if Charlie had to get into the member's locker to replace the member's cleaned golf shoes.

Charlie the locker attendant, not only maintained the locker room spotlessly but also monitored the flat-screen TV behind the bar that served as his desk. These screens showed all of the lockers and rooms associated with the lockers, twenty-four hours a day; even when no one was supposed to be in the locker room, the images were stored in the cloud. Any member who was seen on the screen was tagged by his or her name, even though the images were intentionally blurred to protect the privacy of the member.

Ham took off his shoes and put on his spiked golf shoes. As he walked away, he unconsciously listened for the click as his locker door closed automatically.

Ham walked through the pro shop and waved to one of the golf professionals, Bob Vance, who was behind the desk.

"Hi, Dr. Marks. Your partners are outside. Have a good game."

"Thanks, Bob," Ham said as he walked out to the golf cart that already held his clubs.

The pro's job also included monitoring the screens that showed every hole on both the north and south courses (thirty-six holes). Members' names would label them and the cart they rode in so that the pro on duty would know the position of each member on the course. This way he could contact members through the two-way speaker in the cart if they needed help. Or, if they were moving too slowly for the group behind them, they could be asked to let the faster group play through, in order to maintain the optimum spacing between the groups of players.

No scorecards or pencils were necessary. The scores were kept on the touch screen in each cart, which showed all the players on one hole, the distance of each player's ball to the cup on the green, and the distance to each hazard (water, tree stands, and sand bunkers) from the player's cart.

The scores were automatically calculated with and without the player's handicap (net and gross) and were fed into the main computer, which would calculate each player's handicap. The handicaps were refigured after six rounds of eighteen holes and were e-mailed to the member whether or not his handicap had changed.

Ham checked his clubs and made sure that they were all there. He checked for drinking water on board the cart and then went over to the putting green to meet his three partners.

He shook hands with Ben and Al, and went to shake hands with and introduce himself to Martin Rasher. Rasher, who was on his cell phone, just waved and said loudly into his phone, "Yeah, I got the lunch you made, and don't bother me for the next four hours unless it's an emergency. Okay? Okay!" He hung up and said, "It's the wife. She don't like me to play golf all day. What should I do—stay home with her? Are you kiddin'?! Hey, how 'bout playin' for twenty bucks to the low net? Okay?"

Ham ordinarily didn't like to bet on anything, but the other two men said "Sure," so he agreed with a nod of his head. Ham also made note of the fact that cell phones were not allowed on the golf course, but he hated to make a fuss with Rasher the first time he had met the man. Apparently the other two men felt the same way.

Ham stepped over to the practice area and struck three balls with his driver to warm up. He stretched a bit with the shaft of the club behind his back, took a few more practice swings, and then headed to his cart to drive over to the first tee on the south course for his 9:00 a.m. starting time.

He found Martin Rasher in his cart with his clubs mounted on the rear of the cart.

"Okay, let's go, Doc."

As soon as Ham got his second foot aboard, Rasher jerked the cart forward, throwing Ham back in his seat. When Rasher pulled up behind the cart carrying Ben and Al, he jerked to a stop. Ham decided to hang on to the handhold of the cart—at all times.

Rasher jumped out of his cart and shouted, "Let the games begin." And so they did.

Chapter Three

ALL IS NOT QUIET ON THE FRONT NINE

The USGA allows each player to carry up to 14 clubs in his or her golf bag. Each club has a shaft and a hosel, which connects the shaft to the blade. The blade has a grooved face that strikes the ball, creating spin and giving loft to the ball. Each club—from a driver, which is used off of the tee box, to a putter, which is used on the green—sends the ball a different distance. The loft of each club is the angle between the face of the blade and the shaft. The greater the loft angle, the higher the ball will rise in the air when struck.

The distance the ball will travel when struck by each golf club depends on many factors: the strength of the player, the speed of the stroke, and the skill of the player. It is the responsibility of each player to know the distance he or she can send the ball, starting with the driver and decreasing with each club down to the sand wedge.

The usual loft of each iron club in the bag is as follows: 4 iron—25 degrees, 5 iron—28 degrees, 6 iron—31 degrees, 7 iron—34 degrees, 8 iron—37 degrees, 9 iron—41 degrees, pitching wedge—45 degrees, sand wedge—55 degrees.

The distance the average middle-aged amateur player will send the ball with each club is approximately as follows: driver—230 yards (200 yards for women), 3 wood—210 yards (180 yards for women), 5 wood—200 yards (175 yards for women), 2 iron—109 yards (107 yards for women), 3 iron—180 yards (160 for women), 4 iron—170 yards (150 yards for women), 5 iron—160 yards (140 yards for women), 6 iron—150 yards (130 yards for women), 7 iron—140 yards (120 yards for women), 8 iron—130 yards (110 yards for women), 9 iron—120 yards (100 yards for women), pitching wedge—110 yards (90 yards for women), sand wedge—90 yards (80 yards for women).

A player may substitute a higher-lofted wedge or a so-called hybrid club (part wood, part iron) for another club in his bag, as long as the total number of clubs, including a putter, is at or below fourteen.

The first hole on the south course was a straight 350 yard par 4. The rough and trees lined both sides of the fairway, and sand bunkers on each side lined the elevated green.

The four men decided that they would keep the same arrangement for driving off of the tee for all eighteen holes. The distance of the farthest ball from the hole would determine who played next.

Ben Fowler and Albert Ducasian would lead off. Ham would play third, and Martin Rasher would play last. That meant Rasher had to stand around the tee box for a considerable period of time while the other three players teed off. Unfortunately he had something to say to each player.

Ben Fowler led off. He placed his tee and ball between the two tee box markers, stood astride the ball placement, and made a few practice strokes.

"Watch out you don't stand in front of the tee markers," Rasher said. "I'd move the ball back if I was you."

Ben looked at Rasher, shook his head, and bent over to move his tee and ball back farther behind the tee markers.

"Is that all right with you?" Ben said to Rasher.

"Yeah, that's good," responded Rasher.

Ben approached his ball and struck it. The ball headed straight down the fairway then curved off to the right and landed in the right rough.

"That's a slice," Rasher said. "You can get rid o' that."

Ducasian struck next. His ball went straight down the fairway 170 yards.

"That's okay!" commented Rasher.

"Thanks, Ben," Albert said somewhat sarcastically as he bent down to remove his tee from the ground.

It was Ham's turn next. He struck the ball straight down the fairway, but only 150 yards.

"Jeez, a big guy like you oughta hit the ball farther than that," Rasher commented.

"I'll keep trying," Ham said—and then he immediately regretted that he had responded to Rasher's criticism.

It was Rasher's turn. He approached the ball and swung his driver. The toe of the club hit the ball and sent it screaming off to the right—an obvious shank.

"Mulligan! Mulligan!" shouted Rasher.

"What are you shouting about?" Ham asked.

"I claim a mulligan. I'm takin' anotha shot," explained Rasher.

"Who said you could do that?" Ducasian asked.

"Well, nobody said I couldn't. You guys can do it too, if ya want," Rasher explained as he placed a second ball on his tee.

"Marty, we're playing for money here," Fowler said.

"Dat's okay. I said you could do it." And with that he struck his ball 110 yards down on the left side of the fairway.

"I'm goin' afta my first ball," Rasher told the group.

"Marty, that ball is lost in the bushes," Fowler stated.

"That's all right, I got five minutes ta find it."

Actually the rule stated that he had five minutes to find the lost ball if he planned to use that ball, but Marty had already hit his mulligan and was obviously going to proceed down the course using that ball.

No one said anything, but all three players looked at each other and shook their heads. They all knew this was going to be a very long day.

After five minutes, by his watch, Marty gave up looking for his lost ball. He returned to the cart where Ham was waiting, and they both proceeded to their respective balls.

A little while later all four men had reached the green. Marty had taken three shots to get out of the green-side bunker and, the shouted profanities that had accompanied his first two attempts were unrepeatable.

Ham and Ben Fowler two-putted, while Marty and Albert took three shots to get their ball into the cup.

"Everybody's gotta put their own score in the computer," Marty said to the other three men. They all knew that, and moreover, they all knew that the computer screen in both carts would reflect all the scores.

Ham put in his five, a bogey, and Albert and Ben noted double-bogey sixes. Marty recorded a triple-bogey seven, but the other three men all knew that it had taken him more strokes than that to get his ball into the cup.

The second hole was a short par 3, with the green well below the elevated tee box. Albert made the green in one, while the other three men all needed pitches to get up. Marty was the farthest from the cup, and so he had the honor. He walked around the green, visualizing the grade of the green from all angles. As he did so, he stepped on the line of both Ham's and Ben's putts to the cup—a definite no-no as per normal golf protocol and common courtesy.

"Marty, you're walking all over our putting lines," Ben said, with some disgust.

"Oh yeah? Well, I'm sorry, but I had to figure out how to hit my putt. Anyhow, I didn't make any marks," Marty responded.

After all the players holed out, the quartet moved to the par 5 third hole. This 503-yard hole was a dogleg left, with side bunkers along the fairway and surrounding the green, leaving only a ten-foot strip of fairway leading up to the relatively small green. The flag was placed off to the left in the front third of the green, making the pitch to the flag even more difficult.

Eventually all four men made it to within pitching distance around the green. Ben Fowler, with his ball resting sixty-five yards from the hole, took a pitching wedge out of his bag and struck his ball. The ball flew through the air on a high arched trajectory and came down, striking the flag stick and landing six feet from the hole.

"You struck the stick! That's a two-stroke penalty," Marty shouted.

Albert Ducasian, who hadn't struck his ball as yet, said, "No, Marty, that's only true if you hit the flag stick from on the green!"

"No!" Marty insisted, "Dat's a penalty!"

Ham interjected. "Why don't we ask the pro? Okay?"

"Okay, okay, but I'm sure that's a penalty."

Ham pressed the red button on his cart, and a familiar robotic voice said, "Yes, Dr. Marks, what can I do for you?"

"ARNI, would you please connect me with the pro shop?"

"Of course, Dr. Marks."

In less than three seconds, a voice came through the speaker. "Pro shop, Al speaking."

"Al, this is Dr. Ham Marks. We have a situation here, and we need a ruling."

"Okay, Dr. Marks, what's the situation?"

Ham explained the episode, and the pro said, "There's no penalty there. The penalty only pertains to a shot taken on the green which strikes an unattended flag stick that is still in the hole. Is that a satisfactory explanation for you and your co-players?"

"Yes, thank you, Al," Ham said, knowing that all four men had clearly heard the explanation.

"Is that okay now, Marty?" Ham asked.

"Yeah, I guess so, but I was sure that was a penalty," Marty Rasher said petulantly.

"Okay, we'd all better speed up playing here or we're going to get docked for slow play," Ducasian admonished.

The next five holes went off without a major problem. Marty Rasher continued to comment on each of the other men's shots and continued shouting obscenities when his own shots went awry.

The ninth hole, the final hole on the front nine, was a real challenge. It was a par 5. The fairway curved down and to the right, ending at a small lake. The green was situated on the opposite bank of the approximately fifty-yard-wide water hazard. Ham, Ducasian, and Fowler all placed their third shots within sixty-five yards of the green. Marty Rasher, however, placed his third shot approximately one hundred yards from the green, with the fifty-yard lake intervening.

"It's your honor, Marty," Ham said, bringing the cart alongside Rasher's ball so that he could read the distance accurately on the GPS screen in the cart, which showed the distance to the water and the distance to the flag, which was placed in the front third of the green.

"The GPS says one hundred ten yards," Ham said.

"Yeah, I'll use my six iron," Rasher said.

"You could lay up right in front of the lake," Ham suggested, pointing to a spot on the screen fifty yards closer to the green, making the next shot a fairly simple sixty-yard pitch over water.

"Nah, I can make this shot," Marty said as he approached his ball, six iron in hand. He checked his target—the flag stick 110 yards away—and started his swing. The club struck the ball and sent it well up in the air. As the ball started a downward trajectory, Marty started screaming, "Go, you son-of-a-bitch ball!" No one who could do anything about it heard him, and the ball came down two yards short of the green and struck the water with a small splash.

"Oh shit!, oh shit!, oh shit!," screamed Marty Rasher as he heaved his six iron into the air—which also landed with a splash and disappeared into the lake.

"Marty, you're going to need that club later," Ham said.

"The hell wit' it," Marty blurted out. "Where do I place the ball for the next shot?"

"Well, there's a chalk circle over on the right, in front of the lake, that I think is the drop spot," Ham offered.

"I don't like that spot," Marty said. "I'm gonna find another spot for a drop."

"Why don't we ask the pro," Ham suggested, while Ben and Albert looked on from their cart.

"Sounds like a good idea," Ben contributed, getting a bit exasperated by the "Marty Rasher Show."

Ham hit the red button and directed ARNI to contact the pro; he then explained Marty's predicament.

"Well, if you don't want to use the drop zone, you can determine, as best you can, where the ball crossed the hazard line. Line that point up with the hole, and drop the ball along that line, okay?" the pro explained.

"You understand that, Marty?" Ham asked.

"Yeah, yeah," Marty said, and he proceeded to walk up to the hazard line just before the lake, at the approximate point at which his ball crossed. He turned around and put his arm out and dropped the ball on the fairway.

Rasher took a pitching wedge out of his bag. Ham said, "Are you sure that's enough club, Marty?"

"Yeah, yeah, yeah!" Rasher approached his ball, addressed it, and swung the club. The ball rose high in the air and came down on the green, but instead of moving on toward the flag, the ball bounced backward and rolled slowly, slowly, slowly back into the lake.

"Oh shit! Oh shit! Oh shit!" Marty screamed, and he struck himself in the forehead with the shaft of his club. The blow knocked him to the ground, flat on his back.

"Marty, are you all right?" Ham shouted.

Rasher didn't answer. Ham jumped out of his cart and went over to Rasher's supine body. The other two men had brought their cart over and were also standing over Marty Rasher.

Ham squatted down over Marty as he called his name, and he slapped him moderately hard, first on one side of his face and then the other. Within seconds Rasher's eyes opened and he said, "What happened?"

"You knocked yourself out with your club," Ham said as he helped Rasher sit up.

"Well, shit. I don't remember that. Now whatta we do?"

"Well, I think you ought to sit in the cart for a while, while we finish the hole."

"Didn't I finish?"

"No, Marty, your ball went into the water—again. I think we'll just give you a maximum eight on this hole—okay?"

"Yeah, yeah," Marty said as Ham helped him into the golf cart.

The three men finished the hole and then drove the two carts to the halfway house for a lunch break.

Marty, by this time, was fully conscious but shaking his head as if to clear up some fuzziness before his eyes.

He pulled a brown paper bag out of his golf bag and entered the small eating area, where the other three men had ordered sandwiches and drinks.

"Are you brown-bagging it, Marty?" Ben Fowler asked.

"Yeah, my wife made me a tuna fish sandwich, and I might as well eat it."

"Are you sure your wife's not trying to poison you, Marty?" Ben Fowler said jokingly.

"Naw. She hates when I play golf, but poison my tuna fish, for gawd's sake? Naw!"

The men spent fifteen minutes finishing their snack. During their eating, they discussed their nine-hole scores—minus half of their eighteen-hole handicaps.

Ham, with a twenty-six handicap, took thirteen strokes off his fifty-three score for a forty on the front nine. If he did as well on the back nine, he would score an eighty for the day.

Ducasian came up with an eighty-two, Fowler with a seventy-eight, and Rasher with an eighty-eight.

After a quick trip to the john, all four men mounted their carts and were off to the tenth tee. Martin Rasher had stopped shaking his head but was mysteriously quiet.

25

Chapter Four

RASHER'S SWAN SONG

A handicap in golf is not a burden for less expert golf players to wear around their necks. In fact, the golf handicap, calculated by the USGA and its member clubs in the USA, is used to bring the net scores of bogey players closer to, and even at times above, the gross scores of scratch players. Scratch players, those who play a course at par, have a handicap of 0.

If, for example, a scratch player scores 72 for 18 holes and a bogey player with a handicap of 18 scores an 89, the bogey player wins the match (89-18=71).

Professional golfers are assumed to be scratch players and therefore do not use the handicap system in their tournaments.

As the foursome, in two golf carts, approached the tenth tee, they came to an abrupt stop and observed a strange sight on the tee grounds.

"There's some guys on the tee. They musta snuck on," exclaimed Martin Rasher.

Sure enough, there appeared to be a foursome moving about the tee box—two tall and two short. Strangely, they were not wearing the usual golf apparel seen at Split Rock. They appeared to be wearing white outfits, with white hats having black peaks.

"They must be guests," Ben Fowler opined.

"I'll ask ARNI what's going on," Ham suggested.

"ARNI."

"Yes, Dr. Marks?"

"Who is playing on the tenth tee of the south course?"

"There is no one on the tenth tee, Dr. Marks."

"Not even guests?" Ham asked.

"No, Dr. Marks. I identify only your foursome approaching the tee."

"Thanks, ARNI."

"You are welcome, Dr. Marks. Have a good game." ARNI concluded the conversation and clicked off.

"Well guys, ARNI can't identify who is on the tenth tee. As a matter of fact, he can't see anyone there at all."

"Let's go up and find out for ourselves," said Al Ducasian as he stepped on the accelerator and headed for the tee box, about seventy-five yards away.

Marty and Ham, and Al and Ben, approached the tee box. Marty shouted out, "For gawd's sake! They's birds!" And indeed, the four beings on the tee box appeared to be four swans—two adult and two immature birds. They seemed to have come waddling out of the tee-side pond and were grazing on the freshly seeded grass on the tee box.

As the four men dismounted from their two carts, the birds paid them no attention.

"Shoo! Get away from there!" shouted Rasher, waving his driver in the air.

Ducasian, the farmer, directed his next comments to Rasher.

"Marty, don't threaten those birds. In the first place, it's against the law, and if you hit—or God forbid kill—one of them, you would get put in jail. Second, they are very fierce animals, and the adults will do almost anything to protect their young."

"Oh shit," Marty said, ignoring the admonition, "they're crappin' all over the tee box!" With that statement, Rasher approached the birds waving his long club and shouting, "Go away! Go away!"

Fowler, the lawyer, called out loudly, "Don't do that, Martin!"

But it was too late. Rasher's club passed within inches of the small birds' heads. Immediately a loud hissing began, much like a dozen radiators or teapots going off at the same time.

The adult swan, hissing loudly, came up from behind Rasher and began pecking him fiercely on his bare legs, below his shorts.

"Stop that! Ouch! Stop that!" Rasher cried out as he swung his club rapidly to ward off the attacking birds.

Soon all four birds were on him, and as he turned to get away, he accidently struck one of the adult birds on its large white body.

The bird spread its wings to a span of six feet and hopped into the air like a ground-to-air missile, striking Rasher on the ear with its beak as he was turning away.

Suddenly all four birds started flapping their wings and covered Rasher, pecking him repeatedly from head to toe, with feathers flying everywhere.

The next thing the observing golfers saw was Martin Rasher heading as fast as he could move, with the four birds all over him, toward the pond. And in he went, golf club flying.

But the birds did not stop their attack. They could handle the water much better than Rasher, even though the pond was only two to three feet deep. He was on his hands and knees, while the birds were paddling, swimming, diving, and flying at him, pecking him about the head.

After about thirty seconds, the birds stopped their attack and swam serenely away, the two young birds on the inside and the adults on their right and left flanks.

The three men watching hadn't closed their mouths since the scene began. They watched as the birds swam away from Rasher, who was now lying facedown in the water, motionless, with blood dripping down the back of his head and neck.

Ducasian and Fowler remained speechless, holding on to their cart, staring at Rasher.

Ham, realizing that Marty Rasher was in real trouble, moved quickly. He removed his shoes and socks, rolled up his shorts, and waded into the pond.

He grabbed one leg and one arm and flipped Martin over so that his mouth and nose were no longer underwater. He then placed one hand under Martin's jaw, pulling it forward and opening his airway the best he could in this manner, and began pulling the man, who appeared to be unconscious, toward the edge of the pond.

By this time the other two men had awakened from their shocked stupor, and they reached into the pond to help Ham bring Rasher out of the pond and onto the grass.

Ham, at the point when the other two men began helping to get Rasher out of the pond, noticed the foul odor of the pond water. Initially he thought that he had stepped into a sewer. Then the stench reminded him of water in a flower vase that hadn't been changed in a long time. The pond smelled strongly of ammonia. *Whew! What a stink,* he thought.

"Turn him on his stomach first; let's see if he'll cough up some of that terrible water," Ham instructed.

Ham helped the men turn him on his abdomen with his head turned to one side. Ham then pushed and pounded on his back to see if he could get Rasher to cough up any water.

Then he put his head close to Rasher's and placed his fingers over the carotid artery in his neck.

He rose up and said to the two concerned men around him, "He's got a good pulse, but he's not breathing. Turn him over, and I'll start some CPR."

The men obediently turned Rasher on his back. Ham turned Rasher's head to one side so he wouldn't aspirate anything he coughed up and end up worse than he was right now.

He then straddled Marty, placed one hand on the base of his sternum and his second hand on top of the first, and began to forcefully push on his chest. Within seconds, Rasher began to cough and spit up water, and gag. Ham held Rasher's face to one side until he took a deep breath and began coughing and saying, "What the hell! What the hell! What happened?"

Ham sat him up, patting him on the back, and said, "It's all right, Marty. Those birds forced you into the pond, and you swallowed some of the water."

"Oh shit! Oh shit! That water tastes awful!" Marty said between coughing and gagging.

Ham held a bottle of water up to his lips and said, "Take a little swallow, Marty."

Rasher took a small sip and then grabbed the bottle and began to drink and spit.

"We should call 911," Ben Fowler said.

"No, no, no! That's all I need. My wife should find me in the hospital—after playing golf—she'll kill me! I'm all right now. Just a little nauseated from the lousy water."

"Okay Marty. I'll have the pro shop put the Abington Hospital Emergency Team on call, and we'll see if you need them when we get back to the clubhouse. Is that okay?" Ham asked.

"Yeah, that sounds good. I'll just sit in the cart while you guys play, okay?"

Ham checked with the other two players, and they all agreed.

Ham pushed the red button on his cart and spoke with ARNI.

"ARNI, connect me with the pro shop."

"Right away, Dr. Marks."

"Hello, pro shop. This is John," the next voice said over the cart's speaker.

"John, this is Dr. Marks. We have somewhat of a problem here."

"What's that, Dr. Marks?"

"Well, Marty Rasher fell into the pond by the tenth tee. He swallowed some water, but he says he is all right except for a bit of nausea."

"Well, what would you like me to do, Dr. Marks?"

"He doesn't want to go to the ER now. He'll ride in the cart, and if anything comes up, I'll call you again. But in the meantime, would you call the Abington Hospital ER and put the emergency service on call that we might need them? Otherwise, one of us will drive him to the ER to be checked out when we get to the eighteenth green."

"I'll do that. Thanks, Dr. Marks."

"Thank you, John." He ended the communication. "Okay, all is taken care of. Let's get you in the cart, Marty, and remember, if you suddenly don't feel right, just holler and we'll call the ambulance. Okay?"

"Okay, that's good. Thanks, Ham," Marty said.

With that, the three men helped Marty to the cart. Ham took off Rasher's shoes and socks and wrapped his feet in a club towel. Ham noticed that Marty's left foot was a bit reddened around the heel, but he thought it was just a reaction to something in the pond water.

The other two fellows took Marty's shirt off, helped him dry himself, and wrapped his torso in the club towels.

The three men gave Rasher a final look, and Ham said, "Are you sure you'll be all right, Marty?"

"Yeah, sure. You guys go on and play."

"Okay, guys, let's play," the lawyer Ben Fowler said. "Ham, why don't you take the honor at each tee, and we'll watch Marty as you tee off, and then you can watch over him while Al and I go. Okay?"

"Sounds reasonable to me," Ham said as he got out of his cart, took his driver out of his bag, and headed for the tee grounds between the white markers.

"Oh, and one other thing," Fowler said. "Let's forget about the bet, okay?" Ham and Al nodded in agreement.

And that's how the threesome progressed without delay over the back 9, a par 35: two par 5s, three par 4s, and three par 3s. The eighteenth hole was a par 4.

The three men played with relative intensity, speaking only when necessary. Marty, on the other hand, kept up his bothersome patter: "Ham, you're pickin' your head up!" "Al, you're takin' too long to find your ball!" "Ben, you gotta learn how to use a fairway wood," and so on.

Ham watched over Marty like an attending physician, taking his wrist pulse at each tee box.

Finally the threesome, plus Martin, reached the eighteenth and final hole—a par 4, uphill to the green, a dogleg left, 406 yards to the cup, which was in the left rear of the moderately sized green; sand bunkers surrounded the green on three sides.

Before making his drive, Ham took Martin's pulse and asked him how he felt.

"I'm a little nauseous, an' I got a sore throat," Marty answered with somewhat of a croak.

Ham checked his pulse against his watch: ninety beats a minute—faster than it had been at the seventeenth hole. Also Ham felt a bit of a tremor in Marty's hand. He thought maybe he was cold, and he put another towel around Martin's shoulders.

"Drink a little water, Marty; we're almost back at the clubhouse."

"Okay, Ham. I'm okay," Marty responded.

The three men drove off the tee. Ham and Ben Fowler hit their balls about 150 yards down the fairway. Al's ball curled off to the right and landed in the rough.

"Bring the club back straight and watch the face of the club—that'll get rid of your slice," Marty said to Al, and then he started to cough.

All three men managed to get their second shots on the fairway. Ham and Ben got their third shots onto the green, but at least forty feet from the cup.

Al Ducasian took two shots to get his ball onto the surface of the green.

"You needed a pitch, Al," said Marty. "Where'd you learn to play this game—da boardwalk in Atlantic City?"

Al did not answer. He joined his fellow players and took his first putt. Ham took two putts to hole out, along with Al. Ben Fowler was about to take his third putt. All was quiet, even Marty.

Suddenly Martin cried out, "I need my Ben!"

Quiet descended over the quartet, and the end began.

Chapter Five

DEAD MEN TELL NO LIES

The calculation of an individual's golf handicap is a somewhat complicated undertaking. It should be left to the USGA or the member clubs (for free).

The numerical items used in the calculation include the following: (1) at least five recent 18-hole scores, and (2) the course rating and the slope from each course played.

The course rating of any course is between 67 and 77. The slope rating of a course falls between 55 and 155 and describes the difficulty of a course for a bogey golfer. The average difficulty is a slope of 113.

Your handicap, which varies in time, begins with subtraction of the course rating from each score. Then find the product of each number multiplied by 113. Find the golf differential by dividing each of the calculated five numbers by the slope rating of each course you play. Then take the lowest of the five numbers and multiply by 0.96. Disregard any numbers after the decimal point. This is your handicap.

Got it? No? Well then, leave it to the USGA.

Ham and Ruth entered their own cars at the valet stand in front of the Split Rock Golf Club. Ham always tipped the valet, even though club rules said not to. He felt that it enhanced their meager salaries and also assured that he would get his car first when waiting in a group.

Ruth Marks headed home to Wayne, Pennsylvania. Ham made a stop at the Abington Hospital Emergency Room to see if he could, in some way, aid or comfort Marty Rasher's widow.

She wasn't there. Ham spoke with the nurse receptionist who ordinarily triaged cases for immediate surgery, patients dead on arrival, and walking wounded to their proper places in the large modern emergency complex.

"I'm Dr. Ham Marks" Ham said to the nurse. "I'm an orthopedic surgeon, and I was present when Mr. Martin Rasher passed away and was brought here by ambulance."

"Why yes, Dr. Marks, Mr. Rasher was brought in here. He was placed in a cubicle, and a doctor was called to officially declare him deceased and complete his death certificate."

"Can you tell me the cause of death?" Ham asked.

"No, I can't do that. But I can refer you to the doctor who filled out his death certificate, if you like," the nurse stated.

"Yes, I'd appreciate that. By the way, has the widow viewed Mr. Rasher's body or talked with the doctor?"

"No, Dr. Marks. Mrs. Rasher has not checked into the ER as yet," the nurse answered, checking her answer on her computer.

"Well, I've spoken with her and told her he would be here, so I expect she'll turn up at some time. Would you please leave a message for her that I was here, and leave her my cell phone number?" Ham explained.

"I'll be happy to, Dr. Marks." Ham gave his phone number, and the nurse entered it along with a message that Ham had visited the ER to see Mr. Rasher, for the widow's information.

At that point the nurse's phone rang. She answered and then gave the phone to Ham.

"It's Dr. Alexander, Dr. Marks. He signed Mr. Rasher's death certificate."

"Thank you, nurse. Dr. Alexander, this is Dr. Ham Marks, I'm an orthopedic surgeon at the Philadelphia University Hospital. I was present when Mr. Rasher died. In fact, I even gave him CPR."

"Oh yes, Dr. Marks. I had a note that you were present at the death according to the EMTs. What can I do for you?"

"Can you tell me what you determine to be the cause of death?"

"I'm afraid that will have to be determined by autopsy, doctor. I declared his death due to heart failure and accidental death. The accidental death diagnosis will make an autopsy mandatory."

"Dr. Alexander, would you please do me a favor and have the pathologist send me a copy of the autopsy report. Here is my address and telephone number." Ham provided the relevant information.

"I'll be happy to, Dr. Marks, and thanks for your interest."

"And please call me, or have the pathologist call me, if there are any questions I can help answer. I only knew Mr. Rasher for one day, but as I said, I was present at his demise."

"I will, Dr. Marks, and thank you. I do have the EMT report and the police report, and I assume that the wife will fill in any past medical history. But I appreciate your offer, and I will pass it on."

"Thanks, Dr. Alexander."

"No, thank you, Dr. Marks. Bye." Dr. Alexander hung up.

Ham thanked the triage nurse, reminded her that his phone number was in the computer in case anyone wished to talk to him, and left the ER.

That night, Ham and Ruth went out for dinner. They actually ate out about four nights a week, including eating at the club and at local restaurants. This night they ate at Yin Yang, their favorite local oriental restaurant.

After studying the menu and ordering their favorites—wanton soup, spring rolls, and sweet-and-sour chicken—Ham and Ruth looked at each other and both began to talk at once.

"Ladies first," Ham said gallantly.

"Well, that may be the most excitement we've ever had in one day," Ruth said, shaking her head.

"What about our wedding day?" Ham answered, staying in the gallant vein.

"Oh, Ham. You know what I mean," Ruth said with a chuckle.

"By the way, did you ever get to speak with Mrs. Rasher?" Ruth asked.

"No. She wasn't at the ER. And she never called me, even though I left my number with the nurse," Ham said.

"Well, I hear she is quite a looker," Ruth said, "but that's until she opens her mouth."

"I can certainly attest to the mouth part. I spoke to her on the phone."

"Oh yes, that's right. Well, the girls at the mah-jongg game say that she looks like a movie star but talks like a gangster's moll," Ruth offered.

"Does she play mah-jongg or cards?" Ham asked as the soup and spring rolls arrived.

"I don't think so. But she does come to the club to work out. And the gossip is that she is flirting with a young, good-looking, Asian golf course groundskeeper," Ruth said.

"That's interesting," Ham said with his mouth full of wonton.

"What's more, the girls are spinning the story that the young man is from North Korea," Ruth said.

"North Korea? No, I don't think so," Ham offered.

"Well, the girls think he is, and he's up to no good—particularly fooling around with Mrs. Rasher," Ruth added.

"Well, I'll check around at the pro shop—but North Korea? I'll bet the girls have that wrong," Ham offered as the main course arrived and he moved the chicken and some white rice onto his dish.

"What else are the girls talking about?" Ham asked.

"Oh, I don't know. Oh yes, two of the girls are sure that they are spraying too much insecticide on the grass around the club and golf course," Ruth said.

"Why is that?" Ham queried between mouthfuls of chicken and rice.

"One of the girls, I think it was Ben Fowler's wife, said she was losing her hair—and blamed it on the insecticides. One of the other ladies, I forget her name, said she was getting recurrent rashes on her arms and legs. She was sure it was coming from the golf course. Her dermatologist even agreed with her."

"Now that you mention it, Joe, the valet, had a terrible rash on his arm. He thought he got it from some poison ivy or oak when he parked some cars near the golf course," Ham said.

"See that?" Ruth said, after finishing off a small portion of chicken. "Maybe they aren't all crazy."

"One other thing I just remembered," Ham said thoughtfully.

"What's that, dear?"

"The chef's cat died in the club kitchen. He was perfectly healthy and spent nights outside catching mice. Maybe its death is related to the other problems we've been talking about."

"Who knows?" Ruth said. "Would you like to hear one more little piece of gossip I picked up at the mah-jongg table?"

"Sure, dear, lay it on me," Ham teased.

"Well, Mrs. Fowler really hates Marty Rasher. She called him the "little fat baker," and she didn't care much for Mrs. Rasher either."

"That's interesting, dear. Was there anything else beside Marty's shape and size that bothered her about him?" Ham asked.

"You bet. She was mad as a wet hen about the fact that Marty hadn't paid a bill from her husband for work that he did buying and incorporating his donut stores. I think she mentioned that Marty owed him around $15,000," Ruth said.

"Well, that is certainly interesting. I'm amazed that Ben even played golf in our foursome with Marty, owing him all that money," Ham offered.

"Well, he probably hides his enmity better than his wife does."

"I guess so," Ham said as the waiter brought the check to the table. The food was good, but the restaurant didn't offer coffee or dessert, which Ham rationalized was better for his waistline anyway.

The check was accompanied by two cellophane-wrapped fortune cookies. Ruth opened hers and smiled.

"What's it say?" Ham asked.

"It says, 'You look good and you do good,'" Ruth answered.

"Perfect!" Ham said. "Now let's see what I've got." He broke open the cookie. "'You are in for a big surprise.'"

"Is that good or bad?" Ruth asked.

"I don't know," Ham said as he signed the credit card slip.

Chapter Six

WATER, WATER, EVERYWHERE, BUT DON'T DRINK IT!

Golf is a difficult game. It is a beautiful game played in the outdoors, where one is surrounded by green grass, trees, water, and sand. It is a healthy game, providing exercise even if you ride in a golf cart. In addition, the game requires only a minimal to moderate amount of athletic prowess. Ask some of the octogenarians how they do it.

On the other hand, golf can be an extremely frustrating game. Very few amateur players can ever merit a scratch handicap, no matter what their age or athletic ability in any other sport.

Even a scratch handicap amateur or a professional golfer can have bad days. One day players can be playing below-par golf, and the next day they can be tens of points above par, no matter how they feel or what physical condition they feel they are in.

The game is expensive. It costs tens (sometimes hundreds) of thousands of dollars to belong to a private golf club. Some courses cost over $250,000 to play as a club member.

In addition, most golfers are asked to pay greens fees and golf cart fees each time they play. The golf cart itself can cost several thousands of dollars to own. A full set of golf clubs, plus the bag, can cost well over $1,000. Then there are golf clothes, golf shoes, digital distance measuring devices, and lessons—lots of lessons at $90 to $200 per hour. And, finally, there is the cost of one's time. It takes approximately five hours away from business or one's family to play one 18-hole round of golf.

So why play this frustrating, expensive, time-consuming game? Because it is addictive. One good drive, one twenty-five-foot putt, and you are hooked! You have to play again, and again, and again.

Ham was reviewing the medical history of a patient he was about to examine in his midtown Philadelphia office. The case involved a forty-five-year-old woman who had worked for the US Post Office for twenty-three years, moving mail from a conveyor-type belt to zip code cubicles in a movable cabinet. She was claiming that the repetitive motion she had used in the job for over two decades had injured her hands permanently. She had her attorney claim repetitive stress syndrome (RSS), a medical condition that causes serious, permanent pain and loss of sensation in one's hands. She was unable to continue her work or do normal household activities, and because, she claimed, her federal job was responsible for her clinical condition, she felt the federal government should pay her damages and yearly wages for the rest of her life.

Ham was closely examining her medical record and would examine her carefully to determine whether there could be some other reason for her claim of job-related physical impairment. Was there another non-work-related physical cause of her symptoms? Was she overreacting or even faking her symptoms? Or had she truly been disabled for the rest of her life by her job? This was serious business and could result in up to hundreds of thousands of dollars spent in treating her condition to cure or ameliorate her pain, plus a similar amount to recompense her for her inability to work and earn a living.

As a forensic orthopedic surgeon, Ham did this up to a dozen times each day. His concentration was interrupted by his office manager, Maria, in her long, white lab coat, who entered Ham's office with a fistful of paper pages and said in her pleasant but serious Greek manner, "Dr. Marks, these pages arrived for you via fax. Since they appear to describe the findings of an autopsy on one of your patients, I thought that you should have them right away."

"Thank you, Maria," Ham said as he took the pages from Maria's hand and took a quick look at the cover page.

"Oh, Maria, this is not one of my patients, but it is of interest to me. It is the autopsy report on that fellow, Martin Rasher, who died on the golf course. Remember? I told you about him last week."

"Oh yes, Doctor. Well I'm sure you are interested in the report of his condition after his unusual death," Maria said.

"I sure am. Thanks, Maria."

With that, Maria left his office and Ham turned his chair away from the records on his desk and stopped it under a light in his office ceiling that would allow him to focus on the fine print in the official autopsy report from the Abington Hospital Department of Pathology.

The cover page bore Dr. Alexander's barely decipherable scrawl. It read,

> Sorry for the delay, Dr. Marks. I got this report to you as quickly as possible. Incidentally, Mrs. Rasher showed up at the ER soon after you left. She identified the body as that of her husband but had no questions for me, and she appeared to be noticeably unmoved emotionally over the death of her husband.
>
> If you have any questions for me, just call the hospital and ask for extension 5010.
>
> Joseph Alexander, MD.

Ham turned to the back page of the six-page autopsy report and looked at the "final diagnosis" section. It read as follows: "(1) Cardiac failure (a) mild coronary atherosclerosis (2) Pulmonary congestion (a) basilar lobe pneumonia (b) excess extrapulmonary fluid (3) allergic response (a) periorbital edema—moderate (b) pharyngeal swelling—moderate to severe (4) erythematous skin reaction, left heel (a) subcutaneous eosinophil infiltration (b) small puncture wound, left heel, in center of erythematous cutaneous reaction."

Hmm, Ham thought. *Interesting findings, but no direct connection, objectively, to the dunking Martin Rasher suffered in the foul-smelling pond on the golf course.* There would be a separate toxicology report on Rasher's blood and stomach contents, and on the excess fluid found in his lung cavities, that Ham would have to see at a later time. Ham turned the report back to the cover page and marked in his own hand, "NB, be sure and ask for toxicology and blood and body fluids," as a reminder to himself to ascertain that important information at some later time.

So what did the autopsy show positively as to what caused Martin Rasher's death? Apparently, he hadn't suffered a massive heart attack or stroke (an examination of Rasher's brain tissue hadn't shown any evidence of a bleeding problem—either hemorrhage or thrombosis [blood clotting]). There was evidence of a significant allergic reaction, either to some element or allergen in the fluid Martin had aspirated or to some other allergen that he had inhaled or eaten or taken in somehow through his skin. An allergic reaction was noticeably present—as Ham's wife, Ruth, had noticed—in his periorbital edema, in the swelling of his throat tissues, and in the reaction of his heel skin of eosinophilia (a common microscopic sign of allergic reaction). But what did the puncture wound in his heel have to do with anything? And what had caused it?

So, had Rasher had an anaphylactic reaction to some allergen that caused respiration problems or shock (his blood pressure suddenly falling to zero)? Had he been poisoned? Was his death accidental or intentional? Ham did not have enough information to answer his own questions. But this was the kind of medical mystery that Ham was used to solving, and deep in his gut (or mind) he felt that with time and additional information, he would solve this mystery as well. Was it Ham's responsibility to solve the cause of Rasher's death? No, but it was a challenge, and Ham loved a challenge—particularly a medical challenge.

Ham's intercom buzzed. He punched the intercom button.

"Yes?" Ham queried.

"Doctor Marks, it's Maria. There is a Horsham policeman, Sergeant McGuire, on the phone for you, on line one."

"Thanks, Maria. I'll take the call," Ham replied as he punched the blinking line on his phone.

"Hello, Officer McGuire, nice to hear from you. I was just reviewing the autopsy report on Martin Rasher that I received in a fax today."

"Well, that's interesting, Doctor. I just received the chemical analysis of the water from the golf course pond that Mr. Rasher fell into. Perhaps we should exchange information in this case," McGuire said.

"Absolutely," said Ham. "Mrs. Marks and I are having lunch in the Grill Room of the Split Rock Golf Club tomorrow. Why don't you join us, and we will exchange copies of the info about Martin Rasher then."

"That's fine, doctor. I can't let you buy me lunch, but I will have a cup of coffee with you. How about twelve thirty?"

"Twelve thirty it is, Office McGuire. And by the way, I was interviewed by a Detective Brown a day or so ago. I think he has interviewed my golf partners as well."

"Well, good. I don't have any access to Brown's reports, but, I will speak to him when I turn over a copy of the water analysis and the autopsy report. I'll see you tomorrow, doctor. Bye now."

"Good-bye, Officer McGuire," Ham said as he put down the phone receiver, thinking that Ruth would enjoy being involved in this mystery.

Chapter Seven

NO GOOD DEED GOES UNPUNISHED

Definitions of various subjects concerning the game of golf often range from the sublime to the ridiculous. In the more serious vein are the following:

1. Ace—A hole in one (one stroke of the ball from the tee puts it in the cup on the green). This often results in a celebration, with the golfer either winning a prize or having to pay for alcoholic drinks for everyone, or both.
2. Honor—The golfer with the lowest score on a hole gets to go first on the next hole.
3. Away—The player farthest from the hole, after all players in the group have made their shots, gets to go first in the next round of shots.
4. Attend the flag—As a courtesy, one player in the group or a caddie holds on to the flag in the cup for another player's shot from just off or on the green and removes the flag as that player's ball approaches the cup. When all players are on the green, the flag should be out of the cup so no player's ball might strike the flag stick and incur a penalty.
5. Slice—The ball, having been struck by a player, curves off to the right (for a right-handed player), usually the result of incorrect direction of the blade face or the stroke.
6. Hook—The opposite of a slice.
7. Break—The curved line a ball on the green takes on its way to the cup after being struck by a player (usually with a putter).

8. Chip—A short shot from off of the green that usually bounces and rolls toward the cup.

9. Draw—A ball that turns right to left while in flight (for a right-handed player).

10. Fade—A ball that turns left to right while in flight (for a right-handed player).

11. Divot—Grass and dirt brought up by a club during a stroke.

12. Dogleg, or leg—A jog the fairway takes to the right or left after starting off in a straight direction.

13. Drop—A ball dropped by a player from arm's length and shoulder height after the last ball struck is in an unplayable position or lie.

14. "Fore"—A shout given by a player to warn those in the path of a struck ball to look out for the ball in flight so as to not be harmed.

15. Gimmee—A short putt that is awarded a player by another player without having to strike the ball, but counting as an additional stroke.

16. Medal play—Play in which each stroke is counted and the player with the fewest strokes wins the round.

17. Match play—Play in which the player with the lowest number of strokes wins the hole and the player with the greatest number of holes won wins the match.

18. Mulligan—A shot a player is allowed to replay by the other players in his group.

19. Hazard—Water, sand, or foliage marked by red sticks. Players may not place their club on the surface of the hazard before striking the ball.

20. OB—Out of bounds. The boundaries of the course are marked by white sticks. A player loses a stroke when his ball lands OB.

21. Pin—Short name for the flag stick in the cup.

22. Shank—A ball struck by the hosel instead of the blade of the club that goes sharply to the right.

23. Top—Ball struck above the center, causing it to dive to the ground and roll.

24. Whiff—A complete miss of the ball that still counts as a stroke.
25. Yips—Nervous twitches on a putt that cause the ball to miss the cup.

Ham and Ruth Marks sat at a round, highly polished rosewood table, set for three, in the Grill Room at the Split Rock Golf Club. There were ten tables set for lunch, but only theirs was occupied, and the only other person in the room on this Wednesday afternoon was the bartender, who doubled as the waiter, bringing food and drink to their table.

The bar was also made of highly polished wood. Colorful rugs and golf-related paintings lined the walls. The sun poured in the windows that looked out on the golf course; all in all, it was a very warm and attractive eating place.

"What a beautiful day," Ruth said as she smiled, looking out on the sun-drenched scene. She wore her workout clothes and had just finished a light workout in the exercise room. Ham was in golf clothes, sport shirt and slacks, and spiked shoes. He had spent his time practicing driving and putting. They were eating salads made especially attractive and delicious by Chef Basker.

Ham had a folder on the table that contained a copy of the autopsy report for Martin Rasher. The folder had been prepared to be given to the police officer they were expecting. Ruth had read the report in detail and had already discussed it with Ham, noting that it had confirmed her opinion of a significant allergic reaction in Martin Rasher, which she had noticed in his appearance while she was helping Ham try to revive him.

At twelve thirty on the dot, the bartender's phone rang. He answered, listened, and said "Okay" into the phone before he hung up. He then turned to Ham and Ruth and said, "Dr. Marks, an Officer McGuire of the Horsham police is coming to your table. Okay?"

"That's fine" Ham said.

The officer entered the Grill Room with his cap under one arm and a folder in his opposite hand. "Dr. Marks," he said as he approached.

"Yes, Officer McGuire. Come in and sit down. We were expecting you. You remember my wife, Dr. Ruth Marks?"

"Oh yes. How are you, Dr. Marks?"

"Just fine, Officer McGuire. Why don't you sit down and have something to eat?"

"Thank you, but I've already eaten. I told Dr. Marks I'd join you for a cup of coffee."

"Fine," said Ham. "Joe, would you please bring us three cups of coffee with all the fixin's."

"Sure thing, Dr. Marks. Coming right up."

The policeman sat down and placed his cap and the folder on the table.

"Oh here, Officer," said Ham, handing the policeman his folder. "Here's the autopsy report on Mr. Rasher."

"And here's the report on the analysis of the pond water for you," said McGuire, exchanging folders with Ham.

The group then concentrated on the contents of the two folders as the barman placed the coffee, cream, and sugar on the table.

"I'm not sure I understand all of this, Dr. Marks, but I am sure Detective Brown of homicide will know what it all means."

"Well, basically, Officer," said Ham, "the report shows some excess fluid in the lungs, some coronary artery disease, and an allergic reaction in his eyes and throat, as well as in his foot, where there is a puncture wound. The toxicology report will come later, and I will fax it to you."

"Oh fine, The station's fax number is 610-553-7232. Just send it to my attention."

"Will do, thanks," Ham said as he copied the fax number into his phone.

"Well, do you think the autopsy spells out the reason for Rasher's death?" McGuire asked Ham and Ruth.

"Not completely," Ruth interjected. "Even after we have the toxicology report, we will still most likely have unanswered questions. What do you think of your lab's analysis of the pond water Mr. Rasher swallowed?"

"It contains methane gas, ammonia, sulfur compounds, and some heavy metal content," said McGuire. "It sounds like a pretty toxic mix to me. How do you think that stuff got into the water?" McGuire asked.

"I have no idea," said Ruth.

"Me either," said Ham. "But I am afraid there is going to have to be a considerable investigation here. The club members can't tolerate having a toxic pond like this on their golf course."

"I'm afraid you're right. I'll inform the club management about this. I'm sure they'll want to close off the area near the pond until things are straightened out. They may even want to bring in the Pennsylvania Environmental Protection Agency."

Just then, the bar phone rang and the barman answered. "Okay, okay, I'll tell him." The barman hung up and turned to Ham with a strange look on his face.

"Dr. Marks, the county sheriff is here to see you."

"The sheriff? What does he want, I wonder?" Ham said in the direction of Officer McGuire.

"I have no idea, Dr. Marks. I certainly didn't call him," said McGuire, with a puzzled look on his face.

A uniformed man, dressed in tan, holding his Smokey Bear hat in one hand and a sheaf of papers in the other, entered the room. He was followed by a young man who was similarly uniformed.

"Dr. Ham Marks?," the uniformed man inquired.

"I'm Dr. Marks," Ham said, "How can I help you?"

"Dr. Marks, I'm Sheriff Foster. I have a warrant for your arrest."

"Arrest!" Ham, Ruth, and Officer McGuire said in unison.

"There must be some mistake," Officer McGuire said as he rose from the table. What are the grounds for the warrant? And who issued it?"

"The warrant," said the Sheriff as he perused the sheaf of papers in his hand, "is for murder, issued by the county grand jury and Judge Samuel Warren."

"Murder?!" said Ham in a strangely squeaky voice. "Who am I supposed to have murdered?"

The sheriff looked at the papers again. "Martin Rasher."

"I think there's been a serious misunderstanding, Sheriff. I tried to save Martin Rasher's life, not murder him," Ham responded incredulously.

"I don't know anything about that, sir, but you will have to come with us," the Sheriff said as the young officer approached Ham with handcuffs.

Ham was speechless as his hands were handcuffed behind his back.

Office McGuire spoke up and said, "Mrs. Marks, you should notify a lawyer right away."

Ham came out of his sudden stupor and said, "Oh yes, Ruth, call Ben Snyderman right away and tell him to meet me—where am I going?" he said, directing his question to the sheriff.

"We will take you to a holding area in the county courthouse, where you will wait until you are arraigned before Judge Warren."

"Yes, Ruth. Tell Ben to meet me there. And Ruth?"

"Yes, dear?"

"I guess the Chinese were right."

"What?" Ruth said, thinking, just briefly, that Ham had suddenly lost it.

"Big surprise!" Ham said with a wry smile as he was marched out of the cozy room. Just before he left the room, Ham turned to his wife. "And you'd better notify Linda Carter of the FBI. I have a feeling there is something big going on here."

"Okay, Ham. Don't worry about it. I'll take care of everything," Ruth said.

"I know you will, dear," Ham said as his parting words.

Chapter Eight

SERIOUS, BUT NOT FATAL

Golf is not always a serious, humorless sport. There is often a laughable side to the game, as the following definitions connote:

1. Army golf—One ball hit too far to the left, the next too far to the right, etc.
2. Yasser Arafat shot—Ugly and in the sand.
3. A son-in-law shot—Not all you hope for, but it will have to do.
4. A pharaoh shot—Buried in the sand.
5. A John Wayne Bobbitt shot—a vicious slice, ending up short.

Shortly after returning from the county courthouse, Ham called a "board" meeting. Three men and two women sat around a decorative wooden table in Ham's family room in Wayne, Pennsylvania. The atmosphere was serious. The men included Ben Snyderman, Ham's attorney, and Albert Stern, a criminal attorney Snyderman had brought in for Ham's defense.

The women were Ham's wife, Ruth, and Linda Carter, the Marks's friend in the FBI. Ham had spent the last thirty minutes bringing everyone up to date, as far as the activities of the Split Rock Golf Club were concerned, and the autopsy and pond water analysis reports.

Snyderman explained what had happened when he had reached the county courthouse and got to see Ham.

"Ham had already been booked in, fingerprinted, had his mug shot taken and had given a swab for DNA.

"I read the warrant and asked to speak to the assistant DA, who had taken the case to the grand jury. She was a young lady named Barbara

Merrill. She's a nice lady, a Princeton graduate, and I informed her that Ham and she had that same alma mater. She was interested in that fact and that Ham was a working orthopedic surgeon who had never met Martin Rasher before the day he died while playing golf with Ham.

"She seemed apologetic and explained that she knew nothing of the situation except that she was given the charge to be brought before the grand jury by the DA's office.

"The case revolved around testimony taken from the other two players, Ducasian and Fowler, not under oath. Apparently they could not rule out that Ham held Rasher's head underwater when he jumped in the pond after him, and they also noted that he didn't call 911 after they all dragged Rasher out of the water. The closest they came to a motive for his actions was that Rasher was so annoying to Ham on the golf course that Ham just wanted to shut him up.

"She said that she presented the case to the grand jury at 1:00 p.m. and that the jury members were just hungry and wanted to get out to lunch, so the quickly indicted Ham and went to eat."

The rest of the "board" just sat there and shook their heads. Ruth spoke for the group.

"How could this possibly happen?"

The criminal lawyer, Stern, spoke next.

"Ben explained the situation to me when I arrived about thirty minutes later. Ducasian and Fowler were nowhere to be seen, nor were there any legal representatives for them. I tried calling the numbers that were noted for them, but no one answered the cells. I then got together with the ADA, and she and I went to see Judge Warren. I explained to Ben what my plan was, and he went and told Ham.

"Judge Warren was receptive and listened to my explanation of the situation and that this was a gross legal mistake. I asked that Ham be released on his own recognizance, and Ms. Merrill didn't object.

"The judge took a deep breath and agreed. He instructed me to bring Ham to court for a pretrial conference three weeks hence and instructed the ADA to make sure that Ducasian and Fowler, with their legal representatives, were present at the conference and that she should instruct the legal representatives that their clients were going to have to testify before him, under oath. The judge signed his order, and I took it to the holding area and got Ham out."

Ham said, "It was quite an experience. You really get to feeling like a bad guy real fast under those circumstances, but Ben and Al were just great. I didn't even get to meet the bail bondsman I see on TV. Just as well."

Ruth spoke up. "Ham, why don't you take Linda out to the club tomorrow and go over the scene of the crime—so to speak?"

"Great idea, dear. Is that okay, Linda?"

"Sure," Linda said. "What time do you want me here?"

"Why don't you get here about eleven and we'll head out for lunch in my car," Ham said.

"Fine. I'm sure that death connected to an environmental incident will be enough to get me assigned to this case. Eventually, we will get the Environmental Protection Agency involved. I know the Pennsylvania agency director personally, so I will clue her in as to the situation. She can bring in the federal agency if she wants to."

"Well, gentlemen, it was nice meeting you," Linda said as she arose and shook the hands of the two lawyers. "And thanks for taking such good care of my friend Ham. He does have a penchant for getting himself into trouble."

"He certainly does," agreed Ruth, shaking her head.

Chapter Nine

THE BLAME GAME

The rules of golf are clearly laid out in a publication by the USGA. This publication is given freely to every member of the USGA and the R&A. While there are officially only thirty-four rules to the game, each rule has several additional statements complementing the numbered rule. These rules and additions cover virtually every circumstance that a player may meet when playing the game, either in match play or stroke play. The penalties for breaching each of these rules are clearly spelled out in terms of loss of a hole in match play or loss of one or two strokes by the errant player in stroke play. A few penalties even include disqualification from the current game.

The simple definition of the game as defined by the USGA is as follows: "Playing a ball with a club from the teeing ground into the hole by a stroke or successive strokes in accordance with the rules."

FBI agent Linda Carter arrived at Ham's house on the dot at eleven o'clock. In her navy-blue jacket with white piping and her blonde hair tied up in a ponytail, she looked like a Princeton student on vacation, but Ham knew better. She was an extremely professional FBI agent who could—and had, in Ham's presence—shoot her way out of the most dangerous situation anyone could imagine.

Ham drove his car to the Split Rock Golf Club because his car had been tagged by ARNI, as opposed to Linda's official vehicle. As Ham approached and stopped at the automobile gates of the club, ARNI spoke.

"Good morning, Dr. Marks. I see you have a guest with you." There was not much that ARNI couldn't "see."

"Yes, ARNI, her name is Agent Linda Carter, of the FBI," Ham said.

"Very good, Dr. Marks. Please register Agent Carter at the valet desk and pick up an electronic card for her there. Please return the card on leaving the club."

"Very good, ARNI," Ham said, expecting the gates to open. But they did not.

"ARNI, the gates are still closed," Ham announced.

"I know that, Dr. Marks. I have more information for you."

"What is that, ARNI?" Ham said looking quizzically at Linda, who had just about recovered from her shock at the conversation that was going on between Ham and what was obviously an intelligent computer.

"Dr. Marks, you have been placed on a restricted list. You are not allowed to play golf on either course. The south course has been shut down. Also, you are not permitted to eat in the main dining room."

"Why is that, ARNI?" Ham queried.

"For behavior unbecoming a club member," ARNI answered.

Linda piped up. "Ham, they must have information on your indictment."

"Oh, okay. Well, ARNI, will you let us in?" Ham asked.

"Right away, Dr. Marks. Sorry for the delay." The front gates opened.

Ham drove up to the club, and Linda commented, "Well, that was interesting. A conversation with a very intelligent computer."

"Yes, maybe I should have warned you about that. It is one of the reasons why I joined this club. ARNI pretty much sees and controls everything. Actually, that may help you in your investigation," Ham explained.

"It might well do so, Ham. I'm sure ARNI keeps videos of everything that goes on in the club. I'll ask about that," Linda said.

Ham arrived at an empty valet stand. No Joe.

"I wonder what's happened to Joe. Maybe with the temporarily decreased member activity, the valets don't work all the time. I'll leave the key in the car. I'm sure they'll park the car eventually."

Ham and Linda exited Ham's silver Mercedes, and Linda signed a guest book and took a magnetic card with the word "guest" on it and placed it on her pocketbook, which she wore on a shoulder strap.

"Where shall we go first?" Ham asked Linda.

"Why don't we visit the scene of the crime?" Linda suggested.

"You mean the pond around the tenth tee?" Ham asked.

"Yes," Linda answered.

"Okay. Let's get a golf cart and go out there," Ham suggested.

Ham directed Linda through the club, explaining the functions of each room. Finally, they reached the pro shop.

"Hello, Dr. Marks," John, one of the golf pros, said. "What can I do for you?"

"John, this is Agent Carter of the FBI. She would like to see the site on the south course where Mr. Rasher fell into the pond. Could we use a golf cart for that?"

"Well, doctor, you know that the south course is closed—and that there have been certain restrictions placed on you personally."

"Yes, I know. ARNI explained that to us." Ham turned to Linda and said, "John was the person I talked to via ARNI at the time Marty fell into the pond."

"Oh yes? Well, I would like to talk to you about that conversation sometime—if that is all right with you, John."

"Of course, Agent Carter. You do know that any conversations monitored by ARNI will be stored in our computer system."

"I assumed so. Could I possibly get a copy of the conversations concerning the incident?"

"Certainly, Agent. I'll notify our on-site IT man—actually, it's a woman—June Farley. I'm sure she'll cooperate with you. In the meantime, why don't you use cart number eleven to get out on the course. You can reach me with any questions by just pushing the red button on the cart dash and asking for me."

"Thank you, John. I appreciate that," Ham said.

"Of course, doc. I know it is a very difficult time for you."

"Yes it is. Thanks again," Ham said as he directed Linda out to where the golf carts were parked.

"He's a nice fellow, and he will tell you up front what happened on that day."

"Good," said Linda as she mounted the golf cart and Ham drove off.

As the pair approached the tenth tee, Ham stopped the cart and said to Linda, "Here's where we first saw the birds on the tee. We actually thought they were members dressed in white. We approached the tee and realized we were looking at swans—two adults and two baby birds."

"Okay," Linda said as she and Ham both exited the cart and walked onto the tee.

"Marty was angry about the birds and held his driver in a menacing manner. That's when Ducasian and Ben Fowler warned him about menacing the birds."

"But Marty ignored their warning?" Linda asked.

"Absolutely! He started swinging his club and screaming at the birds. The birds initially backed away but then came at him full force, particularly the adults. Then they forced him into the pond, over there," Ham said, pointing to the tee-side pond.

"It doesn't look very deep," Linda said as she walked off the tee to the side of the pond.

"It isn't," Ham said. "It's only about two feet deep, but the birds kept attacking—forcing Marty facedown in the water by pecking him on the back of the head."

"I'll have to check the autopsy findings to see if any bruises or skin breaks were noted on the back of his head."

"Good idea," Ham said. "Anyhow, after a few seconds, when I saw that Marty was not getting up on his own, I took my shoes and socks off and waded into the pool to help him."

"Are you sure it was just a few seconds?"

"Absolutely—I would say Marty was facedown for less than a minute."

"Maybe the strikes on his head knocked him unconscious."

"It's possible," Ham said. "As soon as I reached him, I turned him over and put my hand behind his head to keep it out of the water. Then I put my other hand under his jaw to keep him from swallowing any more water and started to ease him out of the pond."

"So that's when Ducasian and Fowler saw you place your hands on Rasher's head."

"Yes, exactly. Then they bent over—they didn't enter the pond—and eased him out of the pond. That's when I realized how bad the water smelled."

"Let me try something," Linda said. She walked back to the cart and removed the scorecard from beneath its clip on the steering wheel. As she walked back to the pond, she reached into her shoulder bag and took out a matchbook. Squatting in front of the pond, she dipped the card into the pond and then laid the card on the ground. She held the matchbook in one hand, struck a match with the other, and then lit the card on fire. The card burned for a few seconds and then *whoosh!* The card flashed like a roman candle.

"Wow!" said Ham.

"Nope," said Linda. "Methane."

"Methane?" repeated Ham.

"Yep. That's what makes the water smell. Actually, the methane is odorless but the chemical compound in the pond causes the formation of ammonia gas, and that's what you smell."

"Where does the methane come from?" Ham asked, still somewhat astounded by the fireworks show.

"Underground. It may be from a natural leak in the pond or from contaminated groundwater. It could be caused by the hydraulic fracturing process."

"The what?!" Ham asked.

"Fracking," said Linda. "The fracturing of shale way underground to release natural gas and oil—and methane."

"You know, Linda. Ducasian rents out his farmland for fracking not too far from here."

"Well, we'll have to look into that," Linda said. "But let's finish up here. What happened next, after you and your co-players got Rasher out of the water?"

"Well, let's see. I laid him on his stomach first and turned his head to one side to make sure he didn't aspirate. Then I pounded him a few times on the back to see if he would burp up some water. When that didn't work, I and the other two turned him on his back, and I started some CPR. I had just started when he coughed up water and woke up."

"Then what?"

"Well, we sat him up and talked to him and asked him if he wanted us to call 911."

"You asked him?"

"Sure, he was perfectly lucid. His pulse and respirations were normal, and he said that under no circumstances should we call 911, because, he said, his wife would 'kill him' if she had to come to the ER to get him. He said she would kill him, but I'm sure he was kidding.

"Anyhow, I arranged with John in the pro shop to have the Abington Hospital ambulance on standby if we needed them. Then we wrapped him up after we removed the wet clothes and sat him in my golf cart. I figured I would check his pulse and respiration at each hole on the back nine. If I noted anything going wrong, I would have John send the EMTs right to where we were."

"So then what happened?" Linda queried.

"We played the back nine. Marty kibitzed as usual, and his vital signs were okay—until we reached the eighteenth green."

"What happened then?"

"Well, his pulse went up slightly from eighty to ninety beats per minute, and I thought he was shivering slightly. But he said he felt all right, and he kept calling out to us. In fact, he started saying some strange things."

"Like what?" Linda asked.

"Well, as best I can remember, he yelled out 'Hi, Ben; Hi, Ben' and then 'Hi, happy Ben.'"

"Are you sure that's what he said? Sounds pretty weird," Linda said.

"Yeah, it does. But that's what it sounded like to me," Ham answered.

"Then he was quiet for a few minutes, and that's when Ruth and I found him, unresponsive in the cart and called the EMTs and started CPR right away."

"And he never responded?"

"Nope, and the EMTs were there in five minutes and zapped him with the defibrillator about four times, without any response."

"Huh! And nothing else happened to Marty after the fall in the pond?"

"No, but his condition changed dramatically, and I don't know why," Ham said with a frown.

"Well, let me take another sample of the pond water to my friend in the EPA and then we can get back to the pro shop and see if we can find that North Korean your wife was told about."

With that, Linda took a small plastic bottle out of her shoulder bag, filled it with pond water, and wrote a note on the label before placing it back in her bag.

Then they both remounted the golf cart and returned to the pro shop.

Ham walked into the pro shop and said, "Thanks, John, for letting us use the cart."

"Oh, you're welcome, Dr. Marks. Is there anything else I can do for you?"

"Well, yes. Two things, actually."

"What are they, Dr. Marks?"

"First, will you confirm to Agent Carter that I spoke to you from the golf course when Mr. Rasher got into trouble?"

"Oh yes, sure. Dr. Marks called me and asked me to put the Abington Hospital Ambulance on call for Mr. Rasher. Then he called me again from the eighteenth green and told me to send the EMTs right away, and I told him they would be there in five minutes—and they were, weren't they, Dr. Marks?"

"They sure were, John. And one more thing."

"Yes, Dr. Marks, what's that?"

"Do you have anyone on the golf grounds crew who could be mistaken for a North Korean?" Ham asked, rather sheepishly.

"North Korean? Nooo. Oh, wait a minute! Do you mean Ray Kee? He's a South Korean."

"Well, that must be who these ladies spoke to my wife about. Could we talk to him?"

"Sure, doc. Ray's a great young man. He's actually a South Korean pro golfer. He's trying to get his PGA certificate. Unfortunately, he didn't qualify in Q-school—I think it was a language thing. So he signed on here as a groundskeeper, so at the end of the day he can practice on our course until he is ready to qualify. I'll get him for you; he should be back from lunch now."

"Thanks, John."

"No problem," John said as he disappeared into the depths of the pro shop.

"Well I guess that explains the North Korean thing," Ham said to Linda Carter.

"I suppose so, but it's a pretty silly mistake," Linda said.

At that moment, John returned, accompanied by a tall, slim, handsome, Asian-appearing young man, dressed in tan slacks with a club T-shirt and hat on.

"Dr. Marks and Agent Carter, this is Ray Kee."

"Hello, Ray. Could we talk to you for a minute or two?" Ham said.

"Sure. No problem. What can I do?" Ray said in a thick accent that made his *r*'s and *l*'s sound alike to Ham.

"Well, I'll just step out and let you folks talk," John offered.

"Thanks John." John again left the pro shop.

"Ray, we understand that you are a pro golfer in South Korea. Are you planning to move to the USA?"

"Ah, no. I have wife and daughter in Seoul. I came to get PGA certificate, then I go home. Later, when I can afford, I move to USA with family. But that may be many years," he said in halting but understandable English.

"May I ask you a question, Ray?" Linda said.

"Sure," Ray said.

"Do you know a Mrs. Rasher—the wife of Martin Rasher?"

"Ah, yes. She a very pretty lady. A little crazy, though—I think."

"Why do you say that?" Linda persisted.

"She approach me and act very familiar to me, and she talk very funny."

"I'll certainly agree with that, Ray," Ham said. "I've never met her, but I did speak to her, and she does talk with a significant Jersey accent."

"Oh, I thought she came from other country," Ray said. "She want to take me out for a drink and get to know me better. But I say no, I must stay at club. Then she ask if I know Mr. Martin. I say yes. Then she tell me she is very lonesome when he go to play golf, and maybe I can stay with her when he play golf. I say 'Nooo!' Then she say something very strange."

"What was that, Ray?" Linda asked.

"She ask if I have a beehive on golf course somewhere, and I say no, and she say, 'If you find one, put it near Mr. Martin when he go out next time, because he very allergic to bee sting, and if he get stung, it serve him right.' I never see her after that. I almost forget about her until you bring it up," Ray said, shaking his head.

"Well, thanks for telling us, Ray," Ham said, "and good luck with your PGA registration."

"Thank you, Dr. Marks. Is there anything else you need now?"

"No, not now. Thank you, Ray," Linda said.

"You are welcome," Ray said. "I go back to work now." And he turned and disappeared into the pro shop back room.

"How about some lunch?" Ham said. "I think they'll still let me in the Grill Room."

Both Ham and Linda retraced their steps back to the Grill Room and did enjoy a delicious lunch without interruption.

Chapter Ten

THE WATER DOCTOR

Rule number 1, of the 34 rules of golf, defines the game and prohibits players from changing conditions on the course that might influence the movement of the golf ball while playing a hole. The penalty for breach of this rule is loss of the hole in match play or 2 strokes in stroke play.

Rule number 2 defines actions in match play and concludes that the match is won when one side leads by a number of holes greater than the number remaining to be played (e.g., if team 1 leads by 3 holes over team 2, and there are only 2 holes left to play, the match is over and team 1 wins).

Two days later, the silver Mercedes again approached the entry gates of the Split Rock Golf Club. This time Ham, who was driving, introduced Linda Carter again, and a second lady, Dr. Jane Bromly, the deputy director of the Pennsylvania Environmental Protection Agency, to ARNI.

"Welcome, Dr. Marks, Agent Carter, and Dr. Bromly. Enjoy your day at Split Rock Golf Club." ARNI paused. "And Dr. Marks."

"Yes, ARNI," Ham responded.

"Don't forget to register your guests and return their electronic cards when you leave, Dr. Marks."

"Oh, don't worry, ARNI; I won't forget."

"Thank you, Dr. Marks. You and your guests should have a good day at Split Rock Golf Club." The gates opened.

At the valet stand, Joe was present this time.

"Good afternoon, Dr. Marks," Joe said unsmilingly as he opened the doors for Ham and his guests. "Please have your guests sign in and take their guest cards."

"Joe, are you all right?" Ham asked in his best bedside voice.

"I'm fine, Dr. Marks, but member visits are way down since the south course was closed."

Ham was aware enough to read between the lines that Joe meant "My tips have sucked, Doc, since you closed down the golf course with this cockamamie story about poisoned water."

He said, "I'm sorry, Joe; these ladies and I are trying to fix that."

"Well, good luck, Doc," Joe said as he got into Ham's car and drove off.

Ham watched to make sure Joe wasn't heading toward a berry bush. He reminded himself to tip Joe extra well to keep his silver car away from berry stains.

Linda was dressed in khaki today. Dr. Bromly was dressed in a denim jacket over blue jeans. She was also blonde, but she wore her hair in a pageboy cut. She was tall and slim and serious looking. She wore leather boots and carried a bag with "Dr. Water" written on it in light blue script. This was about as funny as she got. She was, as Ham had learned, a PhD in underground water, and while she didn't actually smile, she seemed primed and ready for the challenge of the poison pond at Split Rock.

Ham had arranged with John for two carts to go onto the south course. He would drive one with Linda, and Ray Lee would drive Dr. Water.

Upon arriving at the pond by the tenth tee, both ladies and Ham approached the water. Dr. Bromly put down her kit, got down on her stomach next to the water, and started dipping her right hand in the water and spilling it back into the pond in front of her nose.

"It is ammonia, all right, produced by methanization," she said as she sat up and opened her "Dr. Water" bag. She took out three capped vials, which she proceeded to fill with the pond water. She then attached a label to each vial and wrote the date and location on each vial.

"There's no question that the horrible smell you were talking about, Dr. Marks, came from a natural reaction to methane in the pond."

"The only question then is, where did the methane come from?" Ham queried.

"The most common source of methane gas in natural ponds is natural underground leakage. But nowadays, the process of hydraulic fracturing, or fracking, for gas and oil is thought by some to produce underground leakage of methane, which then gets into natural underground water and from there into natural springs and drinking water produced from underground water wells. This finding here at Split Rock is certainly worth investigating, and I'm glad you called me on this, Linda."

"Well, it was Ham who got me started on this investigation, particularly since it involved the death of a perfectly innocent civilian," Linda answered.

"I'm not sure I'd call Martin Rasher perfectly innocent, but he sure didn't deserve to die while playing golf," Ham remarked.

"I'll tell you what," Dr. Water easily concluded, "Why don't you and Linda go back to the club and wait for me. I'll get Mr. Lee to take me around to all the ponds and sources of water for both golf courses and the clubhouse. I'll take samples and then meet you at the club for lunch so we can discuss the next steps, okay?"

"That's fine, Dr. Bromly. We'll be in the Grill Room waiting for you," Ham said.

With that, Ham and Linda got back in the golf cart and headed back to the clubhouse. Dr. Bromly explained what she wanted to accomplish to Mr. Lee, and they rode off in a different direction.

An hour later, "Dr. Water" walked into the Grill Room and sat down with Ham and Linda. After all three ordered lunch, Dr. Bromly began her report.

"I'll submit a report concerning the underground water in this club and say that one pond needs to be sealed. And I'll recommend how to do that. In the meantime, I would suggest to the club—and you can carry this message to the board of the Split Rock Club, Ham—to fence the pond and just post signs saying … let's see … something like 'Water Not Safe to Drink.' I think, temporarily, that will prevent anything like what happened to Mr. Rasher from happening again."

Ham piped up. "Well, if that pond is fed by a natural spring, where did the contaminants come from?"

"Oh, Dr. Marks, that's the big question. In situations similar to this one in Pennsylvania, I have found that, theoretically, the two most common causes of this type of underground water contamination, assuming all else to be ruled out, such as cattle feeding in the area, are natural contamination by methane, and the leakage from a hydraulic fracturing, or fracking, process in the vicinity.

"First of all, no other bodies of water contain methane in anywhere near the concentrations of the pond at the tenth tee on the south course.

That includes standing water bodies on the south or north course, as well as the water in the clubhouse.

"As it turns out, the tenth-tee pond is fed by a natural spring. All the other water in the club comes from a series of drilled wells, all of which I have sampled and found safe."

At that point the sandwiches and iced tea arrived, and all three began their lunch.

After a few minutes of munching and swallowing, Dr. Bromly began speaking again.

Ham spoke up. "I've heard something about fracking, Dr. Bromly, but could you tell us a bit more? I'll explain why I'm interested when you finish your explanation."

"Sure. 'Fracking' is shorthand for 'hydraulic fracturing.' It is a way of obtaining oil and gas by breaking up shale deposits deep in the earth by forcing millions of gallons of water and chemicals into the ground under tremendous pressure to break open seams in the shale and release the trapped natural gas and oil. The process has been known about for a long time, but in the last few decades the oil companies have developed methods of horizontal drilling that allow them to begin a well at one site and tap into oil and gas deposits miles away. Anyway, the water and chemicals that are pumped into the ground are also returned with the oil and gas, plus some other unwanted substances, such as methane and some radioactive substances. These are all collected and carried away from the well site and buried safely. Environmentalists are constantly protesting fracking because of these "returns," saying that they are leaking out of the well sites and contaminating groundwater. There are two problems with these protests. First, the environmental departments, both federal and state, have been carefully inspecting each well site for years, and I can tell you, from personal experience, that no groundwater contamination from a fracking drilling site has ever been documented in Pennsylvania in the last ten years. That's important in the overall evaluation of fracking, since the major shale deposit known as the Marcellus Shale Deposit runs right through Pennsylvania, from northeast to southwest, and there are approximately five thousand drilling sites operating in Pennsylvania already, and they are increasing by about two thousand per year.

"Some geologists estimate that the Marcellus tract has the potential to produce five hundred billion cubic feet of gas—enough gas to power all the homes in the USA for the next fifty years. And that doesn't even include the shale deposits in Ohio, the Dakotas, and Texas.

"But back to the groundwater situation that we are concerned with. You see, the drilling goes on thousands of feet below the groundwater level in the earth, and the pipes are all encased in steel and cement throughout their lengths. So there is very little likelihood of a leak into the surrounding groundwater. My job depends on confirming that."

"That's very interesting," Ham said. "And here's why I was so curious about the subject. You see, one of my golf partners, on the day that Martin Rasher died, Albert Ducasian, leased out his farmland in Bucks County to a fracking company. And while he has no reason, known to me, for poisoning the water on the golf course—or killing Martin Rasher, for that matter—he may be scared that the drilling on his land may be responsible for this mini disaster and that he might be subject to large fines or worse."

Dr. Water took what looked like a little red book out of her "Dr. Water" bag and opened it. It turned out to be a mini iPad containing all the known current information about fracking in Pennsylvania.

She pushed and pinched her way around the surface of the iPad and then said, "Oh yes, here it is, Albert Ducasian, five hundred acres in Zion Hill, Bucks County, leased to Recovery Oil Company in 2012. There are now twenty wells on the land. Last inspection one month ago. About time for a new inspection. I'll notify the office to see if we can go up there for a preliminary inspection, even though I'm not the PEPA agent for that county. By the way, that area is rather south of the Marcellus tract, but I suppose that with modern horizontal drilling techniques it would be worth a shot to the oil company."

"It's worth hundreds of thousands of dollars a year to Ducasian," Ham said.

"I suppose so. Would you folks like to join me in the trip up to Zion Hill? It's only about a half an hour away from here. I could pick you up in my van with all of the inspection equipment in it here at the club."

"Sure," said Agent Carter, turning to Ham.

"I'm up for it," said Ham. "If you can, make it next Wednesday, when I don't see patients."

"I'll do that, and I'll also call Mr. Ducasian and tell him that we would like to stop in and see him while we're up there," Dr. Bromly said as she noted the appointment in her iPad.

Chapter Eleven

RETURN TO ZION

Rule number 3 pertains to stroke play. The winner is defined as the competitor who completes the round in the fewest strokes. If handicaps are considered, the competitor with the lowest net score wins.

The failure to complete a hole in the competition results in disqualification. Also, if a player refuses to follow a published rule, he is disqualified. Normally, the penalty for breach of a rule in stroke play is 2 strokes.

Rule number 4 states that each player is allowed no more than 14 clubs in his bag. The penalty for breach of this rule is 2 strokes per hole in which the excessive number of clubs is carried.

Rule number 5 explains that the golf ball used in play must conform to the list of conforming golf balls issued by the USGA. Penalty for breach is disqualification. A ball is unfit for play if it is cut, cracked, or out of shape; in any of these cases, it may be replaced.

If a player lifts a ball in play without announcing that he feels the ball may be unfit for play, he incurs a 1-stroke penalty.

It was Wednesday. It was the end of July. It was hot, and the air-conditioning in the white van with "PA DEP" (standing for Pennsylvania Department of Environmental Protection) painted on the side panels along with the yellow, green, and blue keystone-shaped logo of the department (the three colors signifying the air, land, and water in Pennsylvania), was going full blast.

Ham, Linda, and Dr. Bromly sat in the front seat. Dr. Bromly drove. She had picked up the other two at the Split Rock Country Club at 9:00 a.m. Dr. Bromly was again in Levi's. Linda Carter wore her blue jacket and slacks, and Ham wore a sports shirt, slacks, and a light tan jacket. No one wore good shoes. In fact, Dr. Water wore leather boots.

They were on their way to Ducasian's farmhouse in Zion Hill, Pennsylvania. They were carefully following the GPS attached to the van's dashboard.

"Did you have any trouble with ARNI?" Ham asked Dr. Bromly.

"Oh no. Your instructions were great. I just explained who I was and that I was coming to pick you up, and ARNI treated me like an old friend and opened the gates without hesitation."

"Good!" said Ham. "Now, what's the plan?"

"Well, the visit to the farmhouse is in Linda's and your hands, Ham. I'll be the leader when we get to the fracking site. I called the house, and a housekeeper answered. I explained that we were coming on a courtesy call to speak with Mr. Ducasian before going to the most active drilling site for an inspection. The housekeeper didn't sound too happy about it but said she would inform Ducasian.

"Then I called Recovery Oil and told them I was coming to the drilling site for a brief, but not complete, inspection, and that I was bringing you two. They were very cordial. They want to put their best foot forward when it comes to dealing with the PA DEP. They said they would notify a foreman by the name of Barry Roberts, who would be happy to take us around. Coincidentally, I've reviewed all of the reports on previous inspections, and no significant leaks have been found—that is, no leaks that would affect local or distant groundwater—so Recovery has gotten gold stars from us, so far."

For the first twenty minutes of the trip, the van traveled over smooth highway along Route 476. Then, north of Quakertown, the trio turned onto more rural roads, bumping over potholes and stirring up dust. On one particularly long, straight road with minimal traffic, they spotted a barn-red pickup truck heading their way at a pretty good clip, stirring up a lot of dust. The truck passed them by, and both Linda and Ham spotted three young people in the truck, a blonde young lady with a ponytail was driving. Two tow-headed young men were in the open back of the truck. As the two vehicles passed each other, with the truck traveling much faster than the white van, Ham spoke out.

"Linda, didn't it look to you like one of the boys in the back had a rifle?"

"It sure did, Ham. I can't imagine that that trio is going out hunting right now," Linda answered as she reached into the occult holster she always maintained under her jacket and took out her Glock pistol.

"Whoa! Whoa! Whoa! What is that all about, Linda?"

"Don't worry, Joan. It's just a precaution in case that group decided to come after us instead of some deer," Linda Carter answered.

Ham, who was sitting between the two women in the front seat, said, "You want me to move to the back of the van, Linda?"

"No," Linda answered, "just stay where you are, and Joan, just maintain your present speed. Hopefully we won't see that wild bunch again."

But hope, which usually springs eternal, was somewhere else this morning. The pickup truck made a skidding turn about a quarter of a mile behind the van and started after the van at about sixty miles per hour.

"Uh oh—they're coming back!" Dr. Bromly said, staring into her rearview mirror.

The pickup overtook the van on the two-lane highway. After coming up directly behind the van, the pickup pulled to the left and started running next to the van.

Fortunately, there was no traffic in the opposite direction. This allowed the three young people to run parallel with Ham, Linda, and Dr. Bromly for a few seconds.

Suddenly the young man with the weapon aimed it at the van and pulled the trigger twice. Two big booms resounded through the van. All three occupants ducked at the same time. Dr. Bromly pulled the van onto the shoulder of the road and stopped. Linda Carter leaned out of the passenger-side window and fired off three quick shots from her weapon as the truck drove quickly away.

"Linda, what were you firing at?" Dr. Bromly shouted.

"I was firing well away from the truck. Just to show them we were armed. Maybe that will scare them away from us."

"Well, you accomplished something. They were so shaken up that they ran off the road into a cornfield and just disappeared," Ham said while he took a moment to differentiate the booming of his heart in his chest from any more weapon fire. He recovered enough to look at the others in the front seat and say, "Is anyone hurt? Check yourself out."

All three checked themselves and their clothes to make sure there were no holes in either.

"I'm okay," Dr. Bromly said.

"Me too," Linda said.

"I'm fine," Ham said. "Now what?"

"Well, first let's see what damage was done to the van. Did they hit our tires or engine?"

Everyone piled out of the front seat of the van; Ham and Dr. Water were shaking a bit at the knees.

They looked over the side of the van facing the road and saw multiple holes in the keystone logo of the PA DEP. The tires, engine, and undercarriage did not appear to have been struck by any of the pellets.

"Guess that was a shotgun, Ham," said Dr. Bromly. "He peppered this whole side, but we should still be able to drive. I'd better check the equipment inside." She opened the rear doors and climbed into the van.

"Did anyone get the license number of the truck?" Linda asked.

"I think I did," Ham said.

"What was it?" Linda asked.

"I think it was a Pennsylvania truck license, number "R-F-A-R-M," Ham answered.

"R-F-A-R-M—you mean like short for 'Our Farm'?"

"I guess so," Ham said.

"Well, good work Ham—keeping your head and all," Linda said.

Ham laughed. "I half expected you to shoot to kill, so I was a bit nervous," Ham admitted.

"Oh come on, Ham. I wasn't going to endanger those young kids."

"Those young kids could've killed or seriously injured us," Ham said, shaking his head.

"Well, they didn't. And they didn't wreck any of my equipment either," said Dr. Bromly, stepping backward out of the van's rear door. "So it looks like we can continue our trip."

"Well, we've got some time, so let me call 911 and check in with the local or state police," said Linda.

Linda called and got connected to the nearest Pennsylvania State Police barracks. She explained the situation and provided the truck's license number.

The police dispatcher asked where they were and said a state police car should be with them within ten minutes. He then added, "You don't need medical emergency care, do you?"

"No," said Linda. "All three of us are uninjured, and as far as we can tell, our van is drivable."

The dispatcher thanked Linda and ended the call.

Between five and ten minutes later, the three, while sitting and talking in the van, noted a large cloud of dust moving up behind them. Then they recognized a black police car with flashers on speeding up the road. It pulled in behind the van on the shoulder. A state police officer got out of the car and approached the van, putting on his Smokey Bear hat.

The trio got out of the van and introduced themselves to Officer Watson and proceeded to explain their situation.

Officer Watson then said, "The license plate you reported belongs to a truck owned by a Mr. Albert Ducasian of Zion Hill, Pennsylvania."

"That's very interesting, Officer; we were on our way to Mr. Ducasian's farm when we were fired upon. However, none of the three young people in the truck were Albert Ducasian."

"Perhaps I should accompany you to Mr. Ducasian's' farm—for safety's sake, if no other reason."

"I think that's an excellent idea, Officer," Linda Carter said as she put away her badge, which she had used to identify herself to the state police officer.

"Assuming that no shotgun pellets got into our engine compartment, I think we can make the trip in the DEP van. Is everyone agreed?"

Both Dr. Bromly and Ham nodded in agreement, both feeling a bit safer with the presence of the state police officer on their farmhouse visit.

The police officer said, "Let me call this in to my headquarters. It might be a good idea to have a pair of armed officers meet us at the farmhouse."

Officer Watson returned to his car, reached in the front driver's window, and unhooked his phone. He spoke on the phone briefly, hung up the phone in the car, and approached the trio again and said, "All right, folks. Two police cars will meet us at Mr. Ducasian's house. I didn't think it was necessary to call out a SWAT team."

"Noooo!" the trio echoed in unison, thinking that the last thing they wanted was to be in a middle of a police shootout.

"Why don't I lead the way," Officer Watson offered.

"Fine," said Linda. "Let's go!"

And off they went. The police vehicle with lights flashing, but no siren, led the way, with the shotgun-damaged DEP van following closely behind.

Chapter Twelve

WHEN IS A FARMHOUSE NOT A FARMHOUSE?

Rule number 6 states that a player must announce his handicap before beginning play. If it is determined that he has announced the incorrect handicap, he is disqualified.

If a player is less than 5 minutes late for his starting time, he loses 2 strokes on the 1st hole. If he is greater than 5 minutes late, he is disqualified. There are exceptions to this rule.

The player must be able to identify his ball.

If a player records a lower score on the hole than he actually had, he is disqualified.

Slow play, as determined by the golf committee, may be penalized by 1 or 2 strokes, or even disqualification.

Discontinuation of play, other than when it is allowed by the golf committee, results in disqualification.

If the committee determines discontinuation of the play, the ball may be lifted and replaced in the same spot when play continues.

Penalty for breach is 2 strokes.

Rule number 7 explains that during play, a competitor must not make a practice stroke of the ball or roll the ball on the green. Penalty is 2 strokes.

The police vehicle and the DEP van entered a gate under a sign that read "RFARM, PRIVATE PROPERTY."

"Not a very inviting sign," Ham noted. "I thought that Al Ducasian was a much friendlier man than that—at least for the eighteen holes of golf I played with him."

"Look! There's the truck, or its twin," said Linda, pointing at the barn-red pickup truck parked next to the house.

"You can't have two trucks with the same license number, can you?" Ham asked.

"I don't think so," Linda admitted, noting the "RFARM" license number.

"They must have come through that cornfield after they ran off the road," Dr. Bromly said, pointing to a path of broken cornstalks.

The state trooper had gotten out of his car and was conversing with four other troopers who were standing by their vehicles; the engines were off, but the flashers were on. It reminded Ham of an accident scene, but there was no accident.

"I think we should go in first," Officer Watson told the trio. "We really have to investigate an armed incident here, where a weapon was fired toward another person."

"Fine," said Linda. "We'll be right behind you. And remember, I'm also armed, but I'll keep my weapon holstered."

"I think that's a very good idea," said Officer Watson.

The five state troopers approached the front door of the large clapboard house.

Officer Watson went first, with the other four officers behind him in a semicircle. The four officers had their hands on their holstered but unstrapped weapons, while the fifth man carried a shotgun.

Officer Watson knocked on the front door and said to the men behind him, "Why don't one of you go around back, in case somebody decides to run for it."

With that, the officer with the shotgun and his partner walked around the house—one to the left and one to the right.

Watson knocked again. "State police!" he announced. "Open the door, please!"

For a moment there was no answer, and the two officers looked at each other as if to decide the next move.

Then the door opened a crack, and a voice from inside said, "Yes, Officer, what's the problem?"

"We're here to talk to Albert Ducasian. Would you please open the door and let us in?" Officer Watson said.

The door swung wide open, and a heavyset woman in a maid's outfit—black dress with a white apron—stood back and let the officers,

Linda, Dr. Bromly, and Ham inside. Then she said, "Mr. Ducasian's not here. Is there anything I can do for you?"

"Yes," Officer Watson said. "Could we look around briefly? Then we'll be on our way."

"I guess so," said the maid, who was definitely iintimidated by the quintet that stood in the vestibule of the farmhouse.

The two officers began to nonchalantly, but carefully, stroll around the downstairs rooms, with their hands still resting on their holstered weapons.

Ham and Linda followed behind the state policeman, while Dr. Bromly explained the presence of her trio and presented the maid with her business card.

Ham was looking at some framed pictures on the piano in the living room. He picked one up and approached the maid. "Who are these children?" he asked, pointing to a photo of three ten- to twelve-year-old towheads—a girl and two boys—standing with their arms around each other in front of what appeared to be a swimming pool.

"Oh, that's the grandkids: Sam, Harry, and Judy. Sam and Harry are twins," the maid explained.

"Do they live here?" Ham persisted.

"No, they live in their own house with their mom and dad, about a mile away," the maid said, pointing in the direction of the cornfield outside.

"Were they here today?" Linda asked.

"I didn't see them."

"Did you notice that the truck outside was gone for a while and then was brought back?" Linda asked.

"No, I didn't notice."

"Did you tell Mr. Ducasian about my call?" Dr. Bromly asked.

"Yes, I told him."

"And that the three of us were coming out today?"

"Yes."

"Well, where is he?"

"I don't know. He left the house this morning in his car, and I haven't heard from him since then."

"Could he be out at the drilling site?"

"He could be, but he never told me, so I don't know where he is."

"Well, he's not in the house," said Officer Watson as he was coming down the stairs. "I'm going to leave a ticket here for reckless driving.

It's a $250 fine, and Mr. Ducasian has to show up at State Police Headquarters, which is next to the Zion Hill Courthouse, within seventy-two hours. That's three days. And remember, if he doesn't show, we will be out here to bring him in. And if he isn't here when we come back, we may have to bring you in until we can find him."

"Me! I didn't have anything to do with this hit-and-run or whatever it is."

"I know that, so you explain it to Mr. Ducasian, understood?"

"Yes, yes, I will!" said the somewhat terrified maid.

With that, the officers left the house.

Linda and Ham also gave the maid their cards.

"I'll be back in touch with Mr. Ducasian," said Linda, "so tell him not to leave the area, or he'll have the FBI on his trail. Okay?"

"Yes! Yes!" said the overwhelmed maid, with all the cards and the three-page ticket in her hand.

"Who should Mr. Ducasian contact first?" she asked, looking at all the cards.

"He'd better contact Officer Watson first," said Linda. "I'll catch up with him later."

"Okay," said the maid as she ushered Linda, Dr. Bromly, and Ham out of the door.

Outside of the house, Linda exchanged cards with Officer Watson and told him she would touch base with him within twenty-four hours. She told him he could call her sooner if he needed any more details about the accident.

She also told the officers that the trio was going over to the Recovery Oil drilling site and that if they found Ducasian there, they would let him know.

Officer Watson said, "Thanks, Agent Carter." He then tipped his Smokey Bear hat and took off with the other two police cruisers in a three-car convoy.

Dr. Bromly then said, "Let's find out what goes for a town center here in Zion Hill and have some lunch before we head out to the drilling site. We can call Barry Roberts at lunch and lock down the time of the visit and the exact driving directions."

"Sounds good to me," said Linda.

"Me too," said Ham. "I'm hungry after all that excitement."

Chapter Thirteen

FRACK, BABY, FRACK!

Rule number 8 explains that advice concerning the play of a course may not be given to a player by anyone other than his partner or caddy. Penalty for breach of rule 8 is the loss of 2 strokes.

Rule number 9 states that failure to provide opponents the number of strokes taken, including penalty strokes (even if the penalty is not known at the time), results in loss of the hole.

Rule number 10 explains that honor (first to play) on the 1st hole is determined either by lot or by agreement of the players. On each following hole, honor is determined by the range of net scores on that hole (lowest to highest). If a player goes out of turn at the tee or on the course (being furthest from the cup), he may be asked to replay his shot in the correct position without penalty.

Ham and Linda were crunching bacon-lettuce-and-tomato sandwiches on rye toast when Dr. Bromly sat down at the table in Wendy's Diner.

"Okay. We're all set. Barry Roberts will meet us at site nineteen, the latest drilling site. It will take about twenty minutes to get there from here, and I've got the GPS coordinates for the van. He said to wear shoe covers, since it's pretty muddy out there."

"I've got some work boots in the van," said Linda.

"And I brought galoshes at Linda's insistence," said Ham.

"Well, let's go," said Dr. Water, having finished half of her very large and very delicious BLT.

"I'll bring some great-looking blueberry muffins and some water for the trip," said Linda.

"Here," said Ham, offering his Amex card. "Let me pay for the meal."

"Why don't we let the state foot the bill," Dr. Bromly said. "It's more official that way."

"Okay," said Ham, putting his plastic back in his wallet.

Back on the road, the trio sat in front as the van followed along rural roads, every once in a while passing some very large tanker trucks sitting on the shoulder of the road, their drivers sleeping, eating, smoking, or talking on their dashboard-mounted telephones.

"They're mostly water trucks," Dr. Bromly explained. "It takes literally millions of gallons of water to drill one fracking site."

Finally, at the end of a long, dusty one-and-a-half-lane road, the GPS spoke: "You have reached your destination."

Dr. Bromly brought the van to a stop. The three occupants looked around in some wonderment.

"This looks like a construction site on the moon," Ham said, his head turning from left to right and back again.

Small pickup trucks were parked in a helter-skelter manner, covered with dust. An oil derrick rose in the middle of the scene with men (and probably women) moving around it in white coveralls with white helmets on. Each helmet had "Recovery" printed on it in large block letters. Sizeable tanker trucks were parked at all angles around the derrick and between it and several large tanks sitting on the ground. In addition, a large open container that looked like an above-ground pool, but was more the size of a small lake or large pond, sat in the middle of the muddle.

The liquid filling the above-ground pool did not look at all inviting for a swim.

Large piles of steel piping were stacked at various positions on the ground. At one of these piles, a large piece of machinery was picking up pieces of pipe and transferring them to the drilling derrick.

Two large concrete trucks with their belly-like barrels spinning slowly were also parked at the drill site, like giant spokes in a giant wheel. And there were long heavy-duty hoses everywhere. The only identifier in the whole awesome scene was a small 2' × 2' sign stuck in the ground reading "Recovery Oil, Well Site #19."

Tap, tap, tap. Someone was knocking at the van window. It was a man with a beard, and instead of "Recovery" on his helmet, it said "Boss."

Dr. Bromly rolled down the window. The man stuck his hand into the cab and said, "Hi, I'm Barry Roberts. You must be Dr. Bromly."

"Yes, I am. And this is agent Linda Carter of the FBI, and this is Dr. Ham Marks."

"Hi, folks. Welcome to Recovery Oil's Well Site #19. Why don't you put on your boots and meet me in the office over there?" Barry said, pointing to a small trailer painted blue with "Recovery Oil Company, Inc." painted in orange to make it stand out.

The trio clambered into the back of the van, changed into their boots or galoshes, and exited through the rear of the van. It soon became obvious to all that despite the clear blue skies, the ground was like a muddy marsh after a heavy rain. Once they had stepped through the muck, they entered a brightly lit office.

"Put on these overalls," Barry said, handing each of the trio lightweight blue coveralls. "They'll protect you from any splashes. Also, take one of those helmets." He pointed to white metal helmets on a shelf with "Visitor" in black letters on the front.

"I'll do the talking while we're walking around. So save your questions for when we get back here. I want you to keep your head on a swivel while we're in the field. Watch for trucks moving in and out, watch for pipes swinging in the air, and particularly look for high-pressure hoses on the ground, so you don't trip and fall. Any questions?"

"Nope, let's go," Dr. Water said, the other two nodding in assent.

The drill site was filled with activity and noise; the drilling, the pounding of pipe down the drill hole, the banging of steel pipes against one another, the growling of the concrete mixers, the diesel engines of trucks and other equipment moving about, and the loud voices of the men calling to each other all sounded over the field of mud with thick hoses lying in all directions on the ground.

"The oil derrick is the center of activity," Barry said, pointing at the three-story structure. "The original hole is drilled using the derrick drill. Then steel pipe is delivered to the derrick and forced down the drill hole. The pipe is driven straight down well over one thousand feet, well below the water table level, so that nothing forced down the pipe can enter the surrounding groundwater."

At the word "groundwater," Dr. Bromly's eyes flashed and she looked and listened with even greater concentration, even though she had heard the same recounting of the facts of fracking many times before.

Barry continued. "Then the concrete trucks come in and concrete is poured to line the pipe before new sections of pipe are forced down inside.

"Then comes the feature of fracking which makes it so unique and allows each derrick to produce over twelve times the amount of gas and oil that a straight-drilling derrick would produce. The pipe is directed laterally for over a mile. This can be accomplished in all directions that the geologists have determined contain productive shale formations.

"Once the pipe and concrete have been laid, the water trucks come up. They fill those large tanks over there." He pointed to three large metal storage tanks.

"Then the water is released and goes to those high-pressure pumps, which force over a million gallons of water, under tremendous pressure, down the pipe and concrete system. The water actually does the fracking, or hydraulic fracturing, of the shale layers, which release the gas and oil to return up the pipe system. The pressurized water contains mainly sand to keep the cracks open, but it also contains half of one percent of chemicals and other additives that are used as dissolvers, biocides, breakers, clay stabilizers, corrosion inhibitors, cross-linkers, friction reducers, whetting agents, iron control, non-emulsifiers, pH adjusters, scale inhibitors, and surfactants," Barry said, finishing off with a deep breath and making Dr. Bromly, Linda, and Ham chuckle and give Barry a little clap.

"Thank you, thank you," Barry said with a light bow, "but I'm not done yet. The gas and oil returns up the pipes, with the return water being known as brine. Because of the high salt content and methane gas, along with a small amount of chemicals and radioactive substances, the brine and methane are separated from the gas and oil. The gas and oil are stored temporarily and then are trucked off in tanker trucks to refineries. The methane gas is collected and either burned off"—he pointed to the high towers with flames burning atop—"or are carted away in tanker trucks."

"Is there any leakage of the methane onto or into the ground?" Linda interjected, getting down to the main reason the trio was standing in this muddy field.

Barry answered without any hesitation. "A University of Texas study in September 2013 found that there was an insignificant loss of less than one percent of the returning methane—actually four tenths of one percent—to the air and ground surrounding the fracking site. Not enough to affect the local farmland or drinking water."

Ham looked at Linda, thinking silently, *Well, that just about lets Ducasian off as the golf course water contaminator.*

"The brine," Barry continued, "is pumped away from the site into collecting pools that are gradually trucked away. Once the pumping is completed, the well is capped with pipes coming off to the various collecting sites and the derrick is moved to the next chosen drill site. It takes about one month to complete each drilling site." Barry stopped his tale at this point and asked, "Any questions so far?"

The trio all shook their heads.

"Well then, let's complete the tour and then have a little refreshment in the trailer." The four walked away from the derrick, and Barry pointed out the various collecting sites and trucks doing their specific duties. He also pointed out the various pumps and the brine collecting pool. He admonished them again to watch their step so that no one would trip over the maze of high-pressure hoses strewn all over the site.

Chapter Fourteen

A Summer Shower Brings No Flowers

Rule number 11 states that the player's ball must be teed up within the markers of the teeing ground, but the player may stand outside the teeing ground to tee off. Failure to adhere to this rule may result in disqualification in match play and loss of 2 strokes in stroke play. Accidentally knocking a ball from a tee does not result in a penalty.

Rule number 12 explains that when searching for a ball, sand or loose impediments may be moved from on top of the ball. The player may move the ball to identify it as his own, but he then must replace it in the original position.

Rule number 13 explains that the ball must be played as it lies, even in a hazard (water, sand, or prohibited area), unless the player chooses a 1-stroke penalty and moves the ball according to rules.

When playing out of a hazard, the player is not allowed to touch, with his club, the surface of the hazard until he strikes the ball.

Penalty for a breach is 2 strokes.

As Ham, Linda, and Dr. Bromly carefully sloshed their way back to the company trailer, Ham happened to look up toward the spot where the PEP van was parked and got a small shock.

"Isn't that Ducasian's truck?" Ham said, stopping in his tracks and pointing to a muddy red pickup truck parked about ten yards from the van, near the company trailer.

Both Linda and Dr. Bromly stopped and looked where Ham pointed.

"Could be," said Linda. "Looks like it, but with all that mud on it, it's a little difficult to tell. Let's go check out the license."

The trio was about twenty-five yards from the trailer when they heard a loud cry from one of the workers or inspectors at the site: "Look out above! There's a pressurized leak!"

The trio looked up in the direction of the warning. A torrent of liquid burst forth from the sky and slammed into Linda's chest with crushing force. Like a set of three variable-sized dominos, the trio absorbed the impact of the pressurized flood. Linda was knocked backward but fell into Dr. Bromly, who could not absorb both the force of the water and the body weight of Linda. Both started to go to the ground. Ham, his face blinded by the water, instinctively stabilized himself by moving one leg backward and extending his arms to catch both women. The combined force knocked Ham to his knees, but he kept the women from falling into the mud.

Ham didn't know whether he felt more like Atlas holding up the world or Sisyphus pushing a giant boulder up a hill, but his muscles strained against the combined weight of the two women and the continuing force of the water pouring out of the sky. He was soaked, as were the women. Fortunately they were all wearing coveralls and helmets. The water, which was running off of his helmet and into his face, suddenly stopped. Six workers were immediately surrounding them, helping them stand upright, handing them towels to wipe their faces and hands, which had been exposed to the bitter, salty-tasting flood.

"What was that!?" Ham asked to the helpful workers.

"A hose from a storage tank let go," Barry said. "Are you all okay?"

"Yes, but I did think for a moment we were going to drown," Linda said. "What was that liquid, and how did the leak occur?"

"The liquid was that brine I told you about. There shouldn't be any toxic substances in it, but we've never had a hose let go before. I am so sorry. Let's get you into the trailer and out of those coveralls."

Barry and the trio entered the trailer and immediately started taking off their helmets and overalls. Fortunately they were all fairly dry under the protective outerwear.

A woman with "Medic" written on her helmet entered the trailer. "Everybody okay?" she asked. "Did anyone swallow any of the fluid?"

Ham answered, "I think we're all okay. I didn't swallow any fluid, did you two?" he asked, addressing Linda and Dr. Bromly.

"No," the two answered. "We kept our eyes and mouth closed," said Linda.

"Okay, I don't think you would have ingested any toxic or poisonous substances even if you had swallowed some. There was a very slight amount of radioactivity in the fluid, though, and we should go over you with a detector once you've washed off your face and hands. Why don't you each go into the bathroom and do that? Here are some fresh towels." She handed a towel to each member of the trio.

After all had washed and dried and were sitting in their street clothes in the trailer, the medic produced a small Geiger counter and passed it over each of them. A quiet series of short clicks was heard as the machine was placed over each of the trio, with the most vigorous clicking occurring when the medic scanned their boots (or, in Ham's case, his galoshes).

"Well, are we all glowing?" Ham asked, half jokingly.

"Noooo, you're all fine," the medic said, followed by an audible low whistle caused by the relieved exhaling of the trio. "Even your shoes register lower than normal—normal for the long-term workers around the drill site."

"So what caused the failure? Linda inquired.

"It looks like a hose clamp slipped off a brine tank," Barry said.

"Has that ever happened before?" Linda asked.

"Not that I know of," Barry answered. "And I'm the one who writes up all incidents." He held up a red-bound loose-leaf notebook he had taken from a bookshelf above his desk. "And I have been doing that for a year."

"Could it have been something other than an accident?" Ham asked. "I mean, could it have been done intentionally?"

"You mean could someone have pulled off the hose from the tank? I suppose so, but I can't, for the life of me, figure out why anyone would do something as stupid as that."

Three sets of eyeballs looked at each other.

"Do you know the farmer Ducasian?" Ham asked.

"You mean the landowner?" Barry asked.

"Yes," Ham said. "He drives a barn-red pickup truck."

"Yes, I've seen him and his truck around here every once in a while," Barry answered.

"Did you see him or his truck today?" Linda queried.

"No, I didn't," Barry said in a thoughtful manner.

"We thought we saw his truck onsite a little while ago—license plate reads R-F-A-R-M," Dr. Water interjected.

"Well, I'll ask around if you like," Barry said.

"Yes, that would be fine, and let me know, please," said Linda, giving Barry her FBI card.

"And the two yellow-haired devils," Ham said, "his grandchildren, a boy and a girl."

"Okay," said Barry. "Is there anything else you would like to see while you're here?"

"No thanks, Barry. You've been very helpful," Dr. Water said, handing Barry her EPA card.

"Yes, thanks Barry," Ham said, handing him his card. "Let's go, ladies, before something else happens," Ham said as he exited the trailer door.

Back in the van, heading back to Horsham, Ham related, "I didn't see that red truck of Ducasian's after our soaking."

"I didn't either," Linda said.

"I'm pretty sure it was there, though."

"Well, that was certainly an interesting day," said Dr. Water.

"If you call almost getting killed by a shotgun blast and drowned by radioactive brine interesting," Ham said, shaking his head.

"I think I prefer peace and quiet," Dr. Water contributed.

"I think we ruled out that Ducasian was responsible for poisoning the water on the golf course with his fracking site," Ham said.

"I'm not sure that Ducasian quite believes that," said Linda.

"Or his grandchildren either," Ham added.

Chapter Fifteen

JUSTICE WAS NOT
BLIND THAT DAY

Rule number 14 states that a player must strike the ball with the blade of the club and may not push, scrape, or spoon it.

Unusual equipment must be okayed by the USGA.

The penalty for rule breach is disqualification.

Rule number 15 explains that playing the wrong ball results in a loss of the hole or 2 penalty strokes.

Rule number 16 states that a ball on the putting green may be marked, then lifted and cleaned, and then replaced.

A player may repair hole plugs, ball marks, and other damage.

The surface of the green may not be tested by rolling the ball. No stroke may be made while another player's ball is in motion.

A putt that results in the ball overhanging the hole may be given the time for the player to reach the ball, plus ten seconds. If the ball falls in the cup after this allotted time, a stroke is added to the score.

Rule number 17 explains that the flag stick may be attended or removed before a stroke on anywhere on the course.

The ball must not strike the flag stick when it is attended or when the stroke is made from the green.

Penalty is loss of 2 strokes.

"Albert Ducasian and Benjamin Fowler, please approach the bench and raise your right hands," Judge Walker called out from the raised dais behind his large desk in Courtroom 1 in Norristown, Pennsylvania.

Silence. No movement in the courtroom.

"Ms. Williams," the judge said, addressing the assistant DA, who immediately arose from her seat at the prosecutor's table. "Where are the two witnesses in this case? I ordered you to have them here today."

"I know, Your Honor. My office could not reach either one by phone or by e-mail. The sheriff visited their homes and could not find them. As far as this office knows, neither witness hired an attorney—although, as you know, Your Honor, Mr. Fowler is himself an attorney, licensed to practice before the Pennsylvania Bar."

"Ms. Williams, I will give your side one more chance. If you can produce both witnesses by the time I count to three, we will continue with this case, all right!?"

"Right, Your Honor."

"One, two, three! There being no witnesses here, no witnesses present who can swear to Dr. Ham Marks's guilt in this matter, I hereby dismiss this case—with prejudice! Is that understood, Ms. Williams?"

"Yes, Your Honor." She sat down.

"Dr. Ham Marks, please stand up."

Ham stood behind the defendant's table.

"Dr. Marks, there being no one to testify against you, I have dismissed your case. You may leave the courtroom now, and you will not have to return in this matter. You do not have to consider yourself innocent or guilty. It is as if no case has been brought against you at all. Sorry this court had to trouble you."

"Thank you, Your Honor," Ham said.

"You are welcome," the judge said, and he stood, picked up the papers in front of him, and turned to leave the room.

"All rise," the bailiff cried out. And all did so as the judge disappeared through a door behind his desk.

"Sit here for a minute while I talk to the DA," Al Stern, Ham's attorney, said to him.

He went over to the assistant DA, and they both smiled and shook hands, and Stern had the ADA sign something. Then she packed up her papers and started to leave the courtroom.

As she passed Ham, she smiled and said, "Three cheers for Old Nassau!"

Ham smiled and waved at her as she left the courtroom.

Al Stern returned and sat down. By this time, Ruth Marks, Ham's wife, had joined them, all smiles.

"Well, that was just excellent. I got Ms. Williams to sign your release papers that I had made up beforehand. So you're free to go and forget all about this unfortunate incident in your life. Do you have any questions, Ham?"

"Yes," Ham said, "I do."

"What's that?" Stern asked.

"Was the judge angry at me for some reason? He talked about 'with prejudice.' What was he prejudiced about?"

"No, no. What he said was that he dismissed the case against you with prejudice, meaning that no one can bring that particular case against you ever again."

"Oh, that's good, right?"

"Absolutely," Stern said. "Now, I do have to bring a few things up for your consideration."

"Okay, what are those?"

"Well, do you feel so aggrieved by this legal action that you wish to take a counteraction—like suing Ducasian or Fowler, or the state?"

"No!" Ham said. "This is enough dealing with the legal system, outside of my medical legal practice. Ducasian and Fowler are going to have to work things out for themselves, and I'm not mad at the state," Ham said.

"Well good," Stern said, "Because it would have been a big pain in the ass to do any of that."

"Great," said Ham, "But I do want to thank you from the bottom of my heart for the brilliant legal job you did for me."

"You are welcome. And I plan to do one more thing for you before I send you my bill."

"What's that?" Ham queried.

"I plan to call the president of the board of the Split Rock Golf Club and get all your privileges reinstated."

"That would certainly be worth another nickel," Ham said jokingly.

"Right," said Al. "So Ham and Ruth, be on your way—and be happy!"

"Thank you, Al. We'll have to have you over to the house with your wife for dinner sometime. Okay?"

"Fine, Ruth, you take that up with my wife, Michelle."

"Okay, I will. So long, Al."

"Bye, folks."

They all left the courtroom smiling.

Chapter Sixteen

ALL'S QUIET ON THE SOUTHERN COURSE

Rule number 18 explains that if a resting ball is moved by an outside agency, it must be replaced without penalty.

If the player moves his ball with his equipment, he incurs a 1-stroke penalty (unless it is covered by sand or is moved while removing a loose impediment or a movable obstruction).

Rule number 19 states that a ball that strikes or is stopped by an outside agency must be played as it lies.

It was a lovely morning in early August. Ham and Linda Carter approached the gates of the Split Rock Golf Club in Ham's Mercedes. Ham stopped at the voice box outside of the gate.

"Good morning, Dr. Marks. It's good to see you again," ARNI's mellow (but still somewhat metallic) voice said.

"Well, it's good to be back, ARNI."

"And I see you've brought Agent Carter," ARNI said.

"Yes … that's true, ARNI. How would you know that? I did return her guest tag."

"You certainly did, Dr. Marks. No, I memorized the radio signal from her cell phone. Are you planning on playing golf today, Dr. Marks? I don't have you listed."

"No, ARNI, Agent Carter and I are just here to inspect the water problem on the tenth tee of the south course and then have lunch."

"Oh, I see. Well, Dr. Marks, all of your privileges have been restored, so you can contact me at any time and I will arrange a golf game for you."

"Well, thank you, ARNI. I think I'll try and meet a few more of the golf members before I set up another foursome. Could I play by myself sometime?"

"Of course, Dr. Marks. Just call the club and ask to be connected with me or the pro shop."

"I'll do that, ARNI, thank you."

"Thank you, Dr. Marks. I understand you've done a great service to the club."

"Well, we're not quite done, but I appreciate the thought ARNI."

"Have a nice day, Dr. Marks—and Agent Carter," ARNI said, and he opened the gates.

Ham drove up to the club with Linda just shaking her head.

The valet met them, opened the passenger door, and then ran around to Ham's door and opened that.

"It's good to see you, Dr. Marks. And you, Agent Carter. You know the guest drill. How long will you be here today?"

"We'll have lunch here," Ham said.

"Fine. Just have a member of the staff give me a call when you're ready to go, and I'll have your car here for you."

"Thanks, Joe," Ham said.

"Business must have picked up," Linda said softly.

"Yes, and I wonder what Al Stern told the board to make me such a hero around here," Ham said, mainly to himself.

"I don't know, but don't look a gift board in the mouth, if you know what I mean," Linda quipped.

"Right. We'll pick up your guest tag and we'll head for the pro shop."

As the pair headed through the club, the chef hailed them.

"Dr. Marks," the chef said. "I understand you and your guest will have lunch with us today."

"Why yes," Ham said, still somewhat taken aback as to how his intentions had already been communicated to the club staff.

"If you would like to eat in the main dining room, I'll set you up with a table overlooking the golf course whenever you're ready."

"Why thanks, chef. That would be nice," Ham said, and he kept walking.

The bartender in the clubroom smiled and waved his hand.

"We're not letting any more policemen in here, Dr. Marks," he said with a chuckle.

Finally they reached the pro shop, and Bob, the head pro, greeted them.

"Why Dr. Marks and Agent Carter, it's good to see you again. You certainly got things moving around here. Thank you."

"Well, you're very welcome, Bob—I think. Agent Carter and I would like to borrow a cart for a short while and see how things worked out on the south tenth tee," Ham explained.

"Of course, Dr. Marks. Take number ten; it's right outside the door."

"Thanks, Bob."

"Thank you, Dr. Marks."

Ham and Linda mounted the cart and rolled out to the tenth tee—or where they thought the tenth tee was. Instead they came upon a series of evergreen trees that had been planted in a circular fashion. No elevated tee was in sight. They moved off to the right and came upon a brand-new tenth tee, with its grass properly trimmed and its signage all in place.

"Well look at that!" Ham explained. "They've created a brand-new tenth tee."

"Yes, let's look inside that circle of trees and see what they did with the deadly pond."

They drove up to the trees, dismounted, and squeezed inside the circle. There they saw that the pond had been completely covered with a steel mesh. There were signs on either side of the covered pond that read "Hazardous Water! Stay Away!" with the "Stay Away!" part in bold red letters. Underneath, in smaller (but also red) lettering, the signs read, "Pennsylvania Department of Environmental Protection."

"It looks like Dr. Bromly has done the job," Linda said.

"I wonder why they didn't just fill in the pond?" Ham asked.

"I think that's because it is fed by an underground spring that they can't really bury. The water would just pop up somewhere else," Linda hypothesized.

"I guess so. Good job, I'd say," Ham said.

"Let's go have lunch."

They both got back in the cart and returned to the pro shop.

As they approached the dining room, the maître d' stepped out and said, "Right this way, Dr. Marks." He escorted them to a table by a sunny window looking out over the magnificently kept green golf course. There were just a few other members dining, but Ham and Linda seemed to be getting all of the staff's attention. They ordered drinks, and the chef stepped up to the table and said,

"I'd recommend the shrimp salad today, folks."

"We'll take your word for it, chef—two shrimp salads. Okay, Linda?"

"Fine," said Linda with a smile, appreciating that Ham was certainly back in the good graces of the Split Rock Golf Club. She leaned over toward Ham and said, "You know, Ham, we still have a death on the golf course to explain."

"Yes, I know, but for now let's just enjoy lunch."

And they did. However, as they were finishing up with coffee and delicious small cookies, a staff member approached the table and said,

"Dr. Marks, there's a call for you. Ordinarily we don't allow telephone use in the dining room, but this appears to be an inside call, so I brought you a wireless phone."

"Why thank you," Ham said, and he put the small wireless device up to his ear.

"Hello, Dr. Marks. This is ARNI."

"Yes, ARNI, what can I do for you?" Ham asked.

"Dr. Marks, Charlie in the locker room would like to see you before you and Agent Carter leave the club."

"Why of course, ARNI. Agent Carter and I are just finishing lunch. We should be with Charlie in just a few minutes."

"Excellent," said ARNI. "I'll let Charlie know. Thank you, Dr. Marks."

"Thank you, ARNI." Ham clicked off the phone and handed it back to the staff member.

"Great!" said Linda. "What did the robot computer want now?"

"Charlie, in the locker room, wants to see us."

"Who's Charlie?" Linda asked.

"He's the man who maintains the locker rooms, with the help of a woman staff member for the ladies. He cleans and maintains all the golf shoes and the lockers. Apparently he's found something he wants to talk to us about."

"Okay, I'm ready," Linda said as she arose from the table. "And thanks, Ham, for such a nice lunch."

"You're quite welcome," Ham said as he stood, made a happy wave to the chef, and left the dining room with Linda.

When the two found Charlie, he was working behind the bar that provided an anteroom to the men's and women's locker rooms, which were entered through separate doors.

Charlie would pick up golf shoes from the lockers (the female attendant would deliver the women's shoes), clean them, and then return them to the locker sites.

Ham and Linda introduced themselves to Charlie, a pleasant-looking bald man with a weathered face.

"I have something to show you, Dr. Marks. I found something in Mr. Rasher's shoe. I know what happened to him, and that you were looking into the cause of his death, so I put in a call to you."

"Well, that's good thinking, Charlie. What have you got to show me?"

"Well, Dr. Marks, I was cleaning his shoes—I knew he had died, but I figured someone would clean out his locker, and I wanted his shoes to be clean when that happened. Anyway, while I was cleaning one of his shoes, I spotted something small and shiny in his heel pad inside the shoe. I lifted out the heel pad and found something."

"What was it, Charlie?"

"Let me show you, Dr. Marks."

Charlie turned and picked up a pair of very clean brown-and-white golf shoes off of the shelf behind him and placed them on the bar in front of Ham and Linda. Demonstrating the inside of the left shoe, Charlie said, "You see that little shiny point there?" He pointed to something in the heel pad.

Ham took the shoe and looked closely, then handed it to Linda.

"Don't touch it!" Charlie warned. "It's sharp!"

Ham and Linda looked at each other.

"Here, let me show you." Charlie carefully took the leather heel pad out of the shoe and turned it over. Ham had no difficulty seeing the shiny gold tack head that showed on the bottom of the heel pad.

"How did that get in there, Charlie?" Ham asked.

"I don't know," Charlie said. "Someone had to put it there—and it wasn't me!"

"When would someone have a chance to place that tack in the shoe?" Linda asked.

"Well, after I finish cleaning the shoes, I return them to the floor, under the member's locker. They stay there until the member either puts them away in the locker or puts them on to play golf. I guess someone could get to the shoes while they're still outside the locker."

"Ham, let me have that heel pad," Linda said.

Ham turned it over to her. Linda had already had put on a disposable glove and removed a glassine envelope from her purse. She carefully removed the tack from the heel pad, touching only the edges of the tack head, and placed it in the envelope and sealed it.

"If we're lucky, we can get a thumbprint from the head, and maybe detect some toxic substance on the point. That might help us identify who put it in Marty Rasher's shoe."

"I think I might be able to help in that," Charlie said. "The club has security cameras that allow security and me to see all the lockers from eight p.m. to six a.m. every day. If you contact security, I'm sure they will allow you, Agent Carter, to look at the security tapes from around the last time Mr. Rasher went to play golf."

"Great idea. Thanks, Charlie."

Ham picked up the phone on the bar and dialed 1. After a short ring, a familiar voice answered.

"Hello, Dr. Marks, what can I do for you?"

"ARNI, would you please connect me to the security office?"

"Of course, Dr. Marks."

Almost immediately, another male voice answered: "Security office, Tony speaking."

Ham explained what he wanted to see, and Tony invited him to the office immediately.

"Thank you so much, Charlie," Ham said.

"Oh, you're welcome, and good luck to you and Agent Carter in figuring out what's going on."

Ham and Linda waved to Charlie on their way out of the locker room area and hurried off to the security office, which Ham knew was just beyond the entrance hall of the club.

They were met by a six-foot-tall muscular man with a blond crew cut and the definite look of a former marine (which he was). They explained what they wanted to see to Tony, who sat them down in front of a high-definition twenty-seven-inch computer screen and showed them how to search the locker room tapes for any specific day and time.

Apparently the system used by the club stored all the recorded tapes without recording over them after a period of time.

Linda took over. She was much more attuned to computer screen searching than Ham. She quickly brought up Marty Rasher's locker on the night before the golf game with Ham. She scanned from 8:00 p.m. on. Marty's clean shoes sat below his locker. Nothing happened until 9:00 p.m. At that point a man came into the camera field and sat on the bench in front of Marty's locker. He looked to the right, and then looked to the left. Linda stopped the scan.

"Is that Marty Rasher?" she asked.

Ham looked carefully.

"No." He hesitated. "No, that's Ben Fowler!"

"Fowler, the lawyer?" Linda asked.

"Right!"

"What's he doing in front of Marty Rasher's locker?"

"I don't know. Let's keep scanning," Ham directed.

Linda resumed the scan. Ben Fowler reached down and picked up the left shoe under the locker and placed it on the bench. He took out a vial with an eyedropper in it, and something else out of a "man bag" he had attached to his belt, behind his back.

"Stop!" Ham said. "Can you focus in on what he has in his hand?"

Without answering, Linda struck a few keys, and the image enlarged to ten times its previous size. She focused on the lawyer's hand.

"Is that a tack?!" Ham said.

"It sure is," Linda agreed, and she struck a few keys to start the scan at normal speed and normal size.

Both Ham and Linda watched with their mouths open (Linda looked better with that facial expression than Ham). They watched as Ben Fowler peeled back the heel pad in the shoe, stuck the tack in from the bottom, and then reseated the heel pad.

"Well, I guess we don't have to worry about finding a thumbprint on that tack," Linda said. "But for evidentiary purposes, I'm going to go ahead with it anyway."

Fowler then squeezed the dropper in the vial and took it out.

"Stop!" Ham said again.

"What!?" Linda said as she stopped the motion on the screen.

"See if you can blow up the label on the little bottle."

Linda tried, and they both put their faces within an inch of the screen to see if they could read the commercial label.

Linda said, "I think it says 'Birds and …' That's all I can read."

"That looks about right to me," Ham said.

"I'll have the office search for a company whose name starts that way," Linda said, and she put the scan back at regular size and speed.

Fowler placed a drop of the liquid from the vial on the sharp point of the tack, closed the vial, and replaced the shoe under the locker. Then he looked both ways again and began to finger the code keys on the locker door.

"He's opening Marty's locker!" Ham said. "How can he do that? Each lock has a personal code known only to the member."

"Well, someone must have squealed," Linda said. "I'll bet it wasn't ARNI."

"No, someone who knows Marty well must have told him," Ham said.

At this point Ben stood up and opened the locker door. He searched the locker quickly and then reached in and pulled out a cylindrical object with a red top and yellow base, with red writing on it.

"See what the writing says," Ham directed.

Linda stopped the scan and enlarged the image of the object.

"It says, 'Epi …'" Linda said.

"That's an EpiPen," Ham said. "It's a spring-loaded emergency epinephrine, injector, used if you have an asthma or allergy attack, or want to prevent one from occurring. It probably means that Marty had a specific allergy that could trigger an anaphylactic attack."

"What's that?" Linda asked.

"It's the body's response to the presence of a specific allergen that a person is very sensitive to. His oral pharyngeal membranes swell, his throat closes, and he develops a rapid heartbeat and can go into shock—and die!" Ham explained.

"Do we know what Marty was allergic to?" Linda asked.

"Hmm. Do you remember the conversation we had with the Korean golf pro, Ray Key?"

"Yes, why? What did he say?"

"Don't you remember? He was talking about Marty's wife. She wanted to know if there were any beehives on the course because Marty was allergic—to bees!"

"Well, what do you know? Do you think that the vial from Birds and—Bees!—could have had something like bee venom in it?" Linda queried.

"That would certainly narrow down my search for the company that put out that vial."

"That would go along with some of the symptoms Marty had just before he died," Ham thought out loud."

"Look! He's replacing the cylinder with one that looks just like it!" Linda said, pointing to the screen.

"I'll bet that can is either empty or contains something other than epinephrine," Ham said. Ben Fowler, on the screen, closed the locker door and quickly disappeared from the scene.

"Wow, I guess he didn't know he was being photographed," Ham said.

"The camera must be camouflaged as a lightbulb or a sprinkler head," Linda said. "They're standard ways of hiding security cameras."

"Well, that was quite a show," Ham said. "Let's stop in the pro shop on our way out and find out if Bob knows anything about Marty's EpiPen!"

Linda and Ham thanked the security man, and Linda asked Tony if he could copy the section of tape they had watched and send the copy to her FBI address. Tony said he would. Last stop was back in the pro shop. Bob was back from lunch, and Ham approached him.

"Bob, do you know anything about Marty Rasher using an EpiPen on the golf course?"

"Sure. I don't know what he was allergic to, exactly; I think I remember him talking about bee stings or wasp stings. But anyhow, he always gave me a fresh EpiPen to place in his golf bag before he went out on the course. You know, Marty, he talked a little funny. He said it was his "Appi-pen." It almost sounded like "happy," but I knew what he was saying."

"Happy-pen?" Ham said quizzically. "Marty said, 'Happy Ben, happy Ben' on the eighteenth green. It was just about the last thing he said. Could he have been calling for the EpiPen in his bag, to ward off an anaphylactic attack he felt he was having?"

"Well, if he was, he still would've been in bad shape, even if you had figured that out and given him the pen—after it had been altered by Ben Fowler. This is crazy. What could Fowler have been thinking?"

"Well, we should find out once we get his statement under oath. I'm going to show all this evidence to my boss and see if we can get a federal warrant for his arrest. If not, we may have to go over all this again with the local police, or maybe that Princeton grad ADA."

"You take care of that, would you?" Ham said. "I want to stay as far away from the law as possible."

Linda laughed. "I've got it under control, Ham—not to worry. Let's go, I've got a lot of work to do. Ham, I think we ought to talk to Mrs. Rasher next. She keeps cropping up in this story."

"That ought to be fun," Ham said, thinking of the conversations he had recently had with that strange woman.

Ham picked up the phone and told ARNI to have the valet get his car. By the time the pair reached the front door, the car was there. Ham tipped Joe well. Joe smiled and said, "Thanks, Dr. Marks. I'm glad you're back!"

Chapter Seventeen

THE COURT SPEAKS

Rule number 20 states that when dropping a ball, a player must stand holding the ball at shoulder height and arm's length. When dropping a ball, the original site of the ball must be marked beforehand.

The ball may not be dropped nearer to the hole than the original spot.

The ball may be re-dropped if (1) it comes to rest in a hazard, (2) it rolls out of a hazard, (3) it rolls onto a putting green, (4) it comes to rest out of bounds, (5) it comes to rest where there is still interference from the original condition, (6) it rests more than 2 club lengths from the original spot, or (7) the ball comes to rest nearer the hole than the ball's original spot.

The penalty for making a stroke from the wrong place is 2 strokes.

Ham picked up the receiver on his office phone and pushed the blinking light.

"Hello, this is Dr. Marks."

"Ham … it's Linda."

"Oh, great, Linda, what's going on in the death-on-the-golf-course saga?" Ham asked.

"Do you have a minute or two, Ham? I don't want to interrupt your practice," Linda said.

"No problem, Linda. I'm between patients. Go ahead, spin your tale," Ham directed as he leaned back in his office chair and placed the receiver between his ear and his left shoulder.

"Okay," Linda said.

"Let's start with Al Ducasian and the blonde devils. The state police were able to pick up the farmer at his house and book him for attempted murder and conspiracy to commit murder. They also rounded up the two grandchildren and booked them on attempted murder of a federal officer—yours truly. The judge released all three on $50,000 bond each, which Ducasian put up. They're scheduled for a court appearance in three weeks."

"Okay, that takes care of one of my golf partners. What about Ben Fowler, the lawyer?" Ham asked.

"With the video that I supplied the court, showing him inserting the poisoned tack into Marty's shoe, an arrest warrant for murder was issued. The police couldn't find him at his house, but his wife mentioned that he might be at his hunting lodge in the Poconos."

"And?" Ham said, asking for more information.

"And," Linda went on, "they couldn't find him there either. So since he may have gone across state lines, a federal BOLO was put out for him."

"BOLO? I'm sure your not talking about that Argentinian thing," Ham said.

"No, Ham," Linda laughed. "Sorry for the initials. BOLO means 'Be on the lookout.' It's a warning to both federal and local law enforcement officials—in this case throughout Pennsylvania, New Jersey, New York, and Delaware—to look for Fowler and arrest him if possible."

"Wow, that's quite a manhunt for a lousy golfer," Ham joked.

"It sure is, Ham," Linda commented. "It's a real role reversal for the pair that caused your arrest. The accusers have now become the accused."

"Well, fair is fair, and all that stuff," Ham said.

"I guess you're right, Ham. Now for the final bit of news," Linda said enticingly.

"What's that?"

"I called Mrs. Rasher," Linda said, "and made an appointment to interview her. She resisted at first, but when I said you were coming along, Ham, she agreed. She called you a nice man."

"Well, that's nice. You'll need me as a translator," Ham offered.

"It was difficult to understand her. What is that accent?" Linda asked.

"That, my dear, is Nort Joysee tawk," Ham said.

"Okay, okay, I guess I do need you. Why don't I pick you up this coming Monday at your house?"

"Okay, it shouldn't take much longer than getting to the club, since she lives right there in Horsham," Ham explained.

"All right, Ham. I'll see you about nine a.m. on Monday. Bye now."

"Bye, Linda," Ham answered, and he hung up his office phone.

Chapter Eighteen

THE GOLF WIDOW

Rule number 21 states that a ball on the green may be cleaned when lifted.

Rule number 22 tells us that a ball assisting or interfering with play may be lifted or played with the permission of the other player.

Rule number 23 explains that a loose impediment may be removed, unless the ball and the impediment are in or touch the same hazard.

Rule number 24 states that movable obstructions may be removed if the ball is in or on the obstruction. The ball may be dropped—or, on the green, replaced—as near as possible to the original spot under the obstruction.

A player may take relief from an immovable obstruction by dropping the ball within one club length from the obstruction, but no closer to the hole.

Penalty for breach is 2 strokes.

Linda drove her 2014 Ford Taurus up the Pennsylvania Turnpike.

"This is a nice car," Ham said, looking around and feeling the leather upholstery. "A lot nicer than that tan job you drove the last time."

"Yes, they did a nice job on the styling of this car," Linda said. "It's almost too nice to give to the FBI."

"Well, you deserve it," Ham said.

Linda smiled. "Thanks, Ham."

The pair pulled off the main highway and into the suburban neighborhood of Horsham, Pennsylvania. They stopped in front of a one-story brick home on a three-quarter acre lot. The mailbox at the end of the driveway had "Rasher" in red letters on it, and underneath it read "Home of the Delicious Donut Shoppes."

"I thought the donut shops were a franchise," Ham remarked. "This house certainly isn't the franchise headquarters."

"I think it's just some donut hyperbole," Linda answered.

Linda rang the doorbell, and the first few notes of "We Are the World" sounded.

"More hyperbole?" Ham asked.

"I guess so," Linda said.

The front door opened, and there stood the widow Rasher. Her hair was so blonde that Ham almost had to shade his eyes. She wore a gold T-shirt that barely covered her breasts, which were unusually large, Ham thought. The T-shirt left her midriff exposed. She wore truly short red shorts that actually left uncovered more than they covered. She was standing on four-inch red high-heeled shoes. Her face, on first look, was strangely reminiscent of Marilyn Monroe's, beauty mark and all. Ham appreciated the plastic surgery and surreptitiously searched for the suture lines on her face and behind her ears as she turned to greet Linda.

"Mrs. Rasher, thank you for letting us come to your house and talk to you. I'm Agent Linda Carter with the FBI. I spoke with you earlier. This is Dr. Ham Marks; he was with your husband when he died. I think you have met before."

"No, I talked to the docta, but I nevah met 'im," Mrs. Rasher said in a sultry voice. "Well, come in, come in. Would you like some iced tea? I got some for ya."

"That would be nice; thank you, Mrs. Rasher," Linda said as she and Ham moved into a large living room with walls covered in what looked like red velvet.

The plush carpet was also red, with a gold border. The furniture all had light-colored wood frames, with upholstery in red, softened by red pillows with a gold pattern on them.

With Mrs. Rasher out of the room, Linda turned to Ham and, in a whisper, said, "It looks like the waiting room of a brothel."

"I wouldn't know," said Ham, "but I wouldn't disagree."

Mrs. Rasher returned and set a tray down on a glass table with gold and red cherubs painted on it. The tray held a pitcher of amber fluid with three glasses, a plate with three donuts covered in various high-caloric icings, and two rolled pastries with chocolate and vanilla filling oozing out of their ends.

As she poured the iced tea into the three glasses, Mrs. Rasher said, "Da donuts are from da Delicious Donut Shoppee."

"What about the rolled pastries? Did your husband make those too?" Linda asked.

"No," answered Mrs. Rasher. "That's a gift from someone. Marty tried, but he could never make them. The taste, I mean. He loved the taste, but couldn't ever match it. It really pissed 'im off. Which one would you like?" Mrs. Rasher lifted the plate and offered it to Ham.

"No thank you," said Linda. Ham started to reach for a chocolate-covered donut but then quickly put his hand behind his back and said with a smile, "I'd better not; I'm trying to diet."

"Okay, but if you change your mind, they'll be right heah," Mrs. Rasher said, placing the plate back on the glass table.

"Mrs. Rasher, we're here to—"

"Call me Millie, won't you," Mrs. Rasher said.

"Okay, Millie. Dr. Marks and I are here to try to find out exactly what happened to your husband," Linda explained.

"He died," Millie explained succinctly.

"Yes, we know he died. We just want to find out how he died—what killed him," Linda said.

"He drank the bad water," Millie added.

"Well, yes, he did accidently ingest some of the contaminated water from the golf course pond, but we're not sure that's what caused his death."

"Well, what else could've done it?" Millie asked.

"Well, for example, didn't you threaten to kill him if he continued to play golf as much as he did?"

"Mee! Mee? Kill Mahty—are you kiddin'? I would never do that!" Millie said. "He was my meal ticket, and I ate good!"

"Well, Dr. Marks told me that Martin said to him that you said you would kill him for playing so much golf. Did you say that?"

"Well, okay, I might've said that once. He kept leavin' me all alone for that damn golf, but I was just kiddin'! What, you think I was gonna poison his tuna fish? No!"

"Millie," Ham interjected. "Did you know one of his golf partners, Ben Fowler, the lawyer?"

"Yeah, shure. He is our lawyer, you know—wills and business stuff. He even helped Mahty buy them donut shoppees. We only owned three stores before we moved from North Jersey. Now we own fifteen."

"And did Marty pay Fowler for his legal work?"

"Shur, of course. There was a bill—a big bill."

"And did Marty pay the whole thing?" Linda asked.

"Well ..." Millie hesitated. "Ben charged four thousand each time he helped Mahty buy one of them shoppees. And I think Mahty paid for one of them."

"So Marty still owed him a lot of money, right?"

"Oh yeah. Ben kept cawlin', and cawlin', and writin' letters, but Mahty never answered. He said he'd pay someday. That's how Mahty operated with everybody. He was cheap!"

"And did that make Ben Fowler angry?"

"Oh yeah. He kept threatenin' to sue. But Mahty said he wouldn't, 'cause then he wouldn't get paid. And he didn't."

"But Marty played golf with Ben Fowler. How could he do that if he owed him so much money?" Linda asked.

"Mahty said golf's a fun game. Ben wouldn't get mad playin' golf, and anyway, he said, 'What's he gonna do—shoot me on the golf course?'"

"Hmm. Tell me something, Millie, do you play golf, or swim, or work out at the club?" Linda enquired.

"Shure. I swim and work out. How you think I keep this figure of mine?" Millie said with a smile.

"Do you have a locker at the club?"

"Shure," Millie answered.

"Does it have a combination lock?" Linda asked.

"Shure. It's da same as Mahty's: 1-5-D-O-N-U-T-S. Mahty could never remember, so he'd always call me, and I'd tell 'im."

"Did you ever give your number to anyone else but Marty?" Linda persisted.

"Nooo," Millie said. Then she stopped for a moment and said, "I did have a problem with a bad headache one day in the gym, and I asked a lady to get a pill outta my locker, so I had to give her my numbah."

"Can you remember who that was?" Linda asked.

"Oh, I dunno ... I think it might've been Dottie Fowler."

"Ben's wife?" Linda asked.

"Yeah," Millie answered.

"Mille," Linda continued, "did you know Ray Lee, who worked at the club?"

"Yeah," Millie answered. "A cute guy, North Korean or sumthin', but he shure couldn't speak English good."

"Did you ever ask him about bees or a beehive?" Linda continued.

"Maybe. Mahty was allergic to bee stings, and I may have wanted to know if there were any beehives on the course—to protect Mahty, you know."

"Yes, well, did Ben Fowler know about Marty's allergies to bee stings?"

Millie hesitated momentarily and then said, "Maybe. We may have talked about what cud hurt or even kill Mahty—for our wills and things. But Mahty always had a EpiPen on 'im, so he was protected. Ya know, he jus' had to inject 'imself if he got stung, and then he was good."

"So Fowler knew about the EpiPen also?" Linda stated.

"Well, yeah, I guess so," Millie said.

"Have you seen Fowler since Marty died?" Linda asked.

"No. I didn't need 'im. Mahty told me if anything ever happened to 'im I should trust one of his managers, Joe Torsini, and I did. And he comes every week and brings money from the stores. He's a nice guy—and very cute!"

"Well, what do you do with the money—put it in the bank?" Linda asked.

"No. Mahty didn't believe in banks. I put it in the barbecue pit in the the backyard."

"In the barbecue pit?" Linda repeated incredulously.

"Yeah, shure. That's what Mahty did, so I kept doin' it."

"How much do you have in there?" Linda asked.

"Oh, a lot. I usually don't tell nobody—but you're from the government, so you won't steal it. So I guess I can tell you. There's about one-half million in there."

"Dollars?" Ham asked.

"Yeah, shure. What, you think I got gold bars in there?" Millie said with a chuckle.

"I would suggest you open a bank account and put that money in it. You're going to have a lot of bills to pay. I'll help you set up the account, if you'd like," Linda offered.

"Okay. That'll be nice. But you know that Joe Torsini pays all da bills, even the vig."

"The vig!" Linda and Ham said simultaneously.

"Yeah, shur, Mahty had to borrow money, ya know, to buy the stores. So he had to pay interest."

"How much did he borrow?" Linda asked, holding her breath.

"Well, Mahty told me he needed about forty thousan' for each store," Millie said.

"So that would be about six hundred thousand, right?" Linda said.

"Yeah, I guess that's right."

"And who did he borrow it from, if he didn't trust banks?" Linda asked.

"Oh, Mahty had his own banker, from North Jersey, named Vinnie. I never did get his last name."

"Vinnie from North Jersey? What did he call his bank?" Linda persisted.

"I remember 'im tellin' Mahty to call him a 'nonbank tender of the mortgages,'" Millie said.

"You mean 'a nonbank tender of mortgages'?" Linda asked.

"Yeah, dat's it," Millie said. "He told us that one time he came here to pick up his vig."

"He came here?" Linda asked.

"Yeah, once a mont'. He kept tellin' Mahty to pay off more than the vig, but Mahty jus' said, 'You'll get it, you'll get it.' And that's when Vinnie would give 'im the cannoli. He said it was his mother's recipe. Mahty jus' loved the taste; he said it was a little bittah, but he loved it—until lately."

"Lately?" asked Mark. "What happened lately?"

"Well, Mahty said that he got an upset tummy the last couple a times he ate one, so he didn't eat the last two. That's why I had them for you today."

"Those two rolls—?" Ham said.

"Cannoli," Millie said.

"Those cannoli came from Vinnie when he came for the vig?" Ham asked.

"Yeah, shure," Millie answered.

"Millie, could we take one with us?" Linda asked.

"Shur," Millie said. "Take both. They're startin' to get stale in the fridge. And I don't eat any of that stuff—my figure, ya know. Here, I'll wrap them for you." With that, Millie left the room with the tray. She returned a minute later with the two cannoli wrapped in wax paper, in a brown paper bag, with the logo of the Delicious Donut Shoppe on it.

"Thank you, Millie. Here's my card. Call me if you think of anything else you want to tell me about anything we've discussed today. And I'll call you in a few days to help you set up a bank account for the money in the barbecue pit. Okay?"

"Okay, thanks. And good to see you, Dr. Mahks."

"Good to see you too, Millie," Ham reached out his hand, and Millie took it and shook it gently, not moving the ten-to-twenty-carat stone on the ring on her fourth finger. *Is that real?* Ham thought.

Ham and Linda walked out the door, got into Linda's car, and drove off.

The only thing said on the drive home came from Ham.

"Vinnie and the vig. Doesn't sound good to me!"

"Nope," said Linda. "Me either."

Chapter Nineteen

IS A MURDERER STILL OUT THERE?

Rule number 25 concerns abnormal ground conditions, an imbedded ball, and the wrong putting green.
Rule number 26 concerns the ball in water hazards.
Rule number 27 concerns a ball lost or out-of-bounds, and a provisional ball.

Ham and his wife, Ruth, were eating lunch in the dining room of the Split Rock Golf Club on a beautiful early September Wednesday afternoon. Ham had finished nine holes of golf with three men whom he had just recently met at the club. Ruth had completed a workout with a personal trainer in the club's well-equipped gym room.

They had both showered in their locker rooms and were sitting down for lunch on their day off from medical practice. The golf course murder of Martin Rasher was still unsolved, but Ham and Ruth tried to resume their normal lives and speak of other topics in their busy lives whenever possible. Conversations about the murder were becoming tedious and rather boring, and they had more things to do in their lives than to talk incessantly about the murder on the golf course.

"What a beautiful day," Ruth observed. "Feels like early fall."

"I think we still have plenty of nice days left in the year—at least I hope so. I really enjoy using this club. I'm glad we joined," Ham said, looking out the window at the sun-drenched golf course.

"Me too," said Ruth, "most of the time."

"Well, this was a difficult introductory period," Ham admitted.

"Is that what it was? I call it an unmitigated disaster," Ruth said.

"Well, I guess so, but I think we're pretty much over the hump now," Ham said.

"You think so? Are all the 'players' accounted for?" Ruth asked.

"Well, let's see. We still don't know exactly what or who killed Marty Rasher. Albert Ducasian and Ben Fowler have been removed from the club membership list. ARNI stands guard against them at the gates. Millie Rasher has also resigned from the membership rolls, mainly out of embarrassment—although I thought it would take more than the killing of her husband at the club to embarrass her. Incidentally, remember the cash-filled barbecue pit in the Rashers' backyard that I told you about?"

"Yup," Ruth answered.

"Well, Linda escorted Millie to the bank to open an account. She had over $2 million in that pit."

"Sounds like dirty money to me," Ruth joked.

Ham smiled. "Very funny. I'm afraid that Millie is going to have some visitors from the treasury and justice departments to give iced tea to very soon."

"And don't forget that nice young man Ray Lee," Ruth added.

"Yes, apparently he missed his wife's kimchi and returned to Korea. It's a shame. I've heard he was a fantastic golf player. I would've liked to watch him play," Ham answered.

"Well, you might see him over here in some open golf tournaments in the next few years," Ruth observed.

"You might be right," Ham agreed. "Let's see, what else. Well, Dr. Water, the Pennsylvania EPA expert, feels that it's extremely unlikely that Ducasian's fracking site had anything to do with contaminating the golf course water. It's a shame that Al took it so seriously that he was going to be blamed for Marty's death, and fined and maybe jailed, that he moved to the dark side and got himself fined and arrested."

"Yes, that was dumb," Ruth agreed. "So what's left?"

"Well, the feds have to find Ben Fowler, and then his story will come to an end, eventually. And then there's Vinnie and the vig."

"Oh yes, Vinnie and the vig. Where are you and Linda going with that angle?" Ruth asked.

"I don't know. But I expect Linda will call and tell me sometime soon," Ham answered.

"In the meantime," Ruth suggested, "why don't you and I finish this delicious lunch and go home and take a nap."

"Sounds like a plan," Ham agreed with a smile.

Chapter Twenty

VINNIE AND THE VIG

Rule number 28 concerns unplayable balls.

Rule number 29 concerns rules of threesomes and foursomes.

Rule number 30 contains rules concerning three-ball, best-ball, and four-ball match play.

One week later, Ham got the call from Linda Carter. She asked Ham if he wanted to join her on a visit to Vinnie's home in North Jersey.

"Sure, why not. You've got a gun, right?"

"Yes, Ham, I've got a gun, but I don't think we'll need it. This is just going to be a visit to Vinnie's home, all worked out ahead of time, with no intention of an arrest," Linda said.

"Okay, Linda, it should be fun. When do you want to go?" Ham asked.

"I'll pick you up Saturday morning. Okay?"

"Great, see you then," Ham said, thinking about how he was going to explain this adventure to Ruth.

Chapter Twenty-One

SETTING THE BAIT

Rules number 31 through 34 concern 4-ball stroke play: bogey, par, and Stableford competitions. Also discussed are the committee, and disputes and decisions.

At 9:00 a.m. sharp on Saturday, Linda Carter, driving her tan Ford Taurus, showed up in Ham's circular driveway. Linda honked her horn, and Ham came out of his open front door, calling back to his wife.

"I'll be home before dinner, dear. Bye now."

Ham got into the front seat and buckled up. He was wearing a gray sport jacket over a collared sport shirt and gray slacks. Linda sported her white-piping-trimmed blue jacket and a blue skirt. From experience, Ham knew where she had holstered her Glock pistol.

"Morning, Ham. You look very ... sporty today."

"Morning to you, Linda. It actually took me considerable time to figure out what would be the appropriate dress for a visit to Vinnie's house. I figured not too formal, yet not too informal—after all, it is a business visit on a nonbusiness day. How did I do?"

"I think you hit it right on the head, Ham. Now settle back; we've got about a two-hour drive to Montclair, New Jersey, just outside of Newark. By the way, what did you tell Ruth?"

"I told her the truth—that we were paying a call on Marty Rasher's banker who lent him the money for his donut franchises. I must admit, however, I didn't tell her the banker was probably a made man of the Cosa Nostra. I thought that might be too much information," Ham explained.

"I think you did the right thing, Ham. I don't expect any problems," Linda stated with a fair amount of conviction.

"I personally telephoned Mr. Vincent 'Vinnie the Banker' DeLucca and explained who we were and that we were just gathering information related to the death of Martin Rasher. I told him that since it was only an informal meeting, I didn't think he needed to have his legal representative present. Vinnie said he'd be there anyway."

"Of course, we already have Vinnie under fairly constant surveillance, with his telephones and faxes tapped at his home, office, and in his car. So there's certainly no need for you or me to have any recording devices on our person."

"That's nice to know," Ham said, half sarcastically and half scared out of his wits.

"Well, you see, we're building a major case against Vinnie for money laundering, fraud, and extortion—and those are just the nonviolent charges. But we're still in the evidence-gathering phase of the case, so don't expect anyone to break down any doors with guns drawn while we're there," Linda said with a chuckle.

"Okay," Ham said, without a chuckle.

"So sit back and enjoy the ride. We'll take the Blue Route, Route 95, and the Garden State Parkway and be in beautiful Montclair, New Jersey in just under two hours. I figure we'll have our visit, and then get some lunch on the way back. How's that sound, Ham?"

"Sounds great," Ham said, making himself more comfortable in the Ford's relatively plush front seat.

Linda drove for a while and then said, "I thought I'd fill you in a bit on our Vinnie and his 'family.' Are you interested?" Linda queried.

"Of course I am," said Ham. "I watched every episode of *The Sopranos*."

"Well, this isn't quite the same thing, Ham. *The Sopranos* was fiction—very well researched fiction—but this is real life."

"Okay, shoot! Err, I mean—go ahead and tell me, Linda, I'm all ears."

"Okay, well first, ever since nine-eleven, the FBI has been focused like a laser beam on antiterrorism, as you no doubt know. We've doubled, tripled, and quadrupled our manpower and improved our information-gathering techniques monumentally. But we never gave up on our crime busting.

The FBI has been tracking down criminals in the Cosa Nostra—or the Mafia, or 'the family'—since the days of prohibition, and we put away a lot of bad guys and gals during all those years; and we haven't stopped yet.

We go after murderers, batterers, loan sharks, frauds, and money lenders, and so far the list of cases would fill a library—or, in today's language, a whole bunch of computer servers. So keeping tabs on guys like Vinnie the Banker is everyday business. But the law changes, and we have to keep up with it. Now, murderers are still murderers, and bone breakers are still bone breakers, and loan sharks and money launderers, et cetera. But do you remember what Millie said about Vinnie's vocation?" Linda asked.

"Sure," Ham answered. "She called him a mortgage lender."

"Right," Linda said. "He's a nonbank mortgage tenderer. That's a new term, created under the Dodd-Frank Bill in 2011. Since banks either can't loan mortgage money to small borrowers any more, or don't want to set up their banks under the mountain of regulations needed to loan mortgage money nowadays, the Massachusetts Indian lady, Elizabeth Warren, came up with the concept of the nonbank mortgage tenderer. That's a person who is licensed to give out mortgage money and is only watched over by state agencies and the Consumer Financial Protection Bureau, an independent federal agency in the treasury department that reports only to the Federal Reserve Bank. And how do you think that works out?" Linda asked.

"Not too well, I should imagine," said Ham.

"'Not too well' may be the understatement of the year. So that's why we have Vinnie the Banker, an old Mafia loan shark, shoveling laundered Mafia money out of his nonbank bank, with usurious interest rates that he actually calls 'the vig' to people like Marty and Millie Rasher. Now, Marty knew Vinnie was a 'family' man, but where else was he going to get $600,000, even at rates that may be as high as twenty percent?"

"Well, I can see the perverse logic in that decision," said Ham. "But what about Millie telling everybody that she's only paying the vig to Vinnie? Seems to me that's a dangerous tale to be telling."

"Well, it is. I told Millie to stop talking about it until we could work things out with Vinnie. You see, 'vig,' or 'vigorish,' is an old loan sharking or illegal betting term. It comes from a Russian term meaning 'winnings,' and it's a percentage built into an illegal gambling or borrowing payback rate, over the normal rate, ostensibly for laying the illegal bet or loaning an amount of money that the borrower, or gambler, can't get anywhere else. It's usually about twenty percent. In Vinnie's case, he is making the vig twice, since he's loaning out money that has already been made illegally. It's a well-known mafia scheme."

"So why don't you shut him down and put him in jail?" Ham asked, now just realizing that he was going to meet this really bad guy in person.

"Oh, we will," Linda said. "But we're putting together a much bigger case than just Vinnie. You see, in this loan-sharking endeavor, Vinnie is just shark bait."

"Oh," said Ham, not knowing whether to be more or less scared at that answer.

For the rest of the trip, Ham and Linda just listened to Satellite Radio and watched the GPS as they drew nearer and nearer to Montclair, New Jersey.

Chapter Twenty-Two

THE SHARK'S LAIR

Additional details describing rules 1 through 34 may be found in *Rules of Golf*, published in 2011 by the USGA and R&A Rules Limited, a copy of which may be obtained through the website www.USGA.org, or by becoming a member of the USGA.

At 11:10 a.m. Linda pulled the car into a circular driveway in front of a large stone-and-clapboard house in Montclair, New Jersey. The lettering on the mailbox read "DeLucca."

"Nice house," said Ham looking about. Reminds me of the house in the—"

"It does a bit," Linda said, breaking into his sentence. "Pure coincidence, I'm sure."

Linda turned off the car's engine and opened the driver's door. Ham opened the passenger door and stepped out. Both of them closed their doors simultaneously.

Before they could take another step, they both felt a pipelike object being stuck into their kidney area on one side of their back. Linda knew what the object was; Ham just guessed.

"Don't make anotha move. Just show us who you are!" one of the pipe wielders said in a Jersey accent.

Linda was prepared and handed over her special wallet with her FBI badge in it. Ham was not prepared. He fiddled with his wallet from his rear pocket and showed the man behind him his AMA card.

"Agent Linda Cahta and Dr. Mahks. Okay, we knew you was comin'," the man behind Linda said. "Now I jus' gotta pat you down for guns."

"I don't think that's a good idea," Linda said firmly. "I do have a service weapon on me, but I assure you it will not be removed from its holster during the time of our visit with Mr. DeLucca. Dr. Marks is unarmed."

"My orders is to pat you down," the man behind Linda said.

Linda was standing with her hands about shoulder height on each side. Her next movements occurred with such blurring speed that Ham felt as if he were watching the type of movie in which the violent action is filmed so rapidly that the viewer can't follow it.

Linda dropped one hand and twisted in place, striking the man holding the weapon behind her on the wrist, relieving him of his weapon with her opposite hand, and ending up holding his arm in an arm bar behind his back, and holding his weapon against his forehead with the other hand.

"Now, why don't we all forget about weapons and go and visit Mr. DeLucca. Okay? Ham, would you please give me the weapon the gentleman behind you is holding?"

Ham turned, took the rough-looking man's handgun, and handed it to Linda, all before his legs had a chance to give way.

Linda said "Thank you" and let go of the arm of the man in front of her. She lowered the weapon from his forehead; unloaded both semiautomatic weapons, dropping the cartridges on the driveway; gave the empty weapons back to the two astounded guards; and said, "You can pick up the rounds later. Now let's go and see Mr. DeLucca."

The two overly muscular but well-dressed men holstered their empty weapons and led the way up the front stairs and in through the front door of Vinnie's house.

Ham and Linda were met in the hallway by a slim man with a tanned and wrinkled face. He was wearing a white shirt, a gray sweater vest, gray slacks, and brown tasseled loafers without socks.

"Mr. DeLucca, this here is Agent Linda Cahta and Dr. Mahks."

"Yes, yes, I know. I saw them introduce themselves to you outside, Sam. Come in, come in, folks. Have a seat." He indicated the plush sofa and chairs in a nearby living room.

"Can I get you anything to drink? Coffee, tea, water, something stronger?"

"No, thank you, Mr. DeLucca," Linda answered, sitting down with Ham on the sofa. "We'll just be here for a short time."

"Vinnie. Please call me Vinnie. Everyone calls me Vinnie."

"That's all right, Mr. DeLucca," Linda said. "Dr. Marks and I just want to touch base with you about your business dealings with Mr. Rasher. You see, Dr. Marks was there when Mr. Rasher died. By the way, is your legal representative here today?"

"No, Agent Carter. I took your word that this would be an informal meeting and that there was no need for my lawyer to be here. Those lawyers charge too much anyway," DeLucca said with a smile. "So what would you like to know? All the dealings I've had with Mr. Rasher are well documented, you know."

"I'm sure they are, Mr. DeLucca. I understand you dealt with Mr. Rasher as a mortgage bank," Linda stated.

"Oh no you don't. You can't trick me," DeLucca said with an unpleasant smile. "I am registered with the State of New Jersey as a nonbank mortgage tenderer. All nice and legal."

"Yes, I do know that. I understand that Marty Rasher, over a period of time, borrowed $600,000 from you, or your nonbank bank. Is that correct?"

"Yeah, that's right. I backed his purchases of his fifteen donut shops."

"And then you allowed him just to pay the interest on the loan. Why was that, Mr. DeLucca?" Linda asked.

"Well, basically, I liked the little guy. He made me laugh," DeLucca said, this time with a true chuckle.

"That's a very nice sentiment, but not very businesslike," Linda persisted.

"No, no it wasn't," DeLucca admitted. "But I would've gotten around to persuading him to pay back some of the principal pretty soon. I didn't expect him to die on the golf course, for God's sake!"

"Yes, I'm sure of that," Linda commented. "What was the gift of the cannoli all about?"

"Oh that. Well it was sort of a spoof on Marty. I bought them here in town, and they did taste like my mother's recipe, but Marty could never make them like that, and he loved the taste."

"Did you personally add anything to the recipe?" Linda probed.

"Me?! What do I look like, a baker, for God's sake? No, I didn't add anything to the recipe. I bought a dozen at a time, and me and my family would polish off eleven of them, and one I carried personally to Marty."

"Well, that was very nice of you," Linda said, with hidden sarcasm.

"Yes, I suppose it was," DeLucca confirmed.

"What do you expect to do about Marty's widow, now that Marty is no longer around?"

"I sent her a note, ya know, but no cannoli. She doesn't like them—thinks they'll ruin her figure. They probably would," DeLuca said with a laugh. "I haven't seen her since Marty died. I do business with one of Marty's managers, who runs the shops now. I think I can work out an arrangement with him."

"Good," said Linda. "I'll tell her not to worry about it."

"Yeah, yeah you do that," DeLucca said.

"Well, thank you, Mr. DeLucca. That's all I have. Ham, do you have any questions?" Linda said, turning to Ham.

"Err, no, I don't think so. Thanks for asking," Ham said, as if he were just waking from a coma or at least a long sleep.

"Well then, I think that ends our visit, Mr. DeLucca."

"Vinnie, please."

"All right, Vinnie. Thank you for your hospitality."

"You are welcome," Vinnie said as he ushered Linda and Ham out of the front door with the bulky guards right behind them.

Halfway to the car, Linda turned to one of the guards and said, "You guys having trouble with rats? I thought I saw one outside of the house."

"No, no," the guard said, turning back to the front of the house. "We took care of them weeks ago."

"Oh, maybe I was mistaken. It could have been a squirrel," Linda said as she got into the car with the guards holding the doors open for her and Ham to enter. With the doors closed, Linda rolled down the window and said, "Thank you, gentlemen. And don't forget to pick up the shells from your guns. Wouldn't want the neighborhood kids finding them." And with that she drove away, rolling up the window.

For the first few miles, all was quiet in the car. Then Ham blew out a breath slowly and said, "Whew. That was some adventure!"

"Adventure?" Linda responded. "Ham, that was just a site visit. But I'm glad you were there. You defused what could have been a very contentious situation."

"Well, glad to have helped. Now, let's go have lunch!" Ham suggested.

Chapter Twenty-Three

WHO DID IT, OR DIDN'T DO IT?

While the rules of golf are sometimes difficult to remember, they are always available in the *Rules of Golf* booklet or at the local pro shop. Golf is a sport that offers outdoor exercise, enjoyment, and conviviality among friends. So play golf whenever you can, and just enjoy yourself.

Ham enjoyed these get-together dinners, where he brought together all of the important individuals who were involved in one of his serious puzzle-solving adventures.

A beautiful table had been prepared by Chef Basker and his staff. Ruth had written out place cards for herself and Ham; Linda Carter; Jane Bromly; Ben Snyderman and his wife, Julia; and Al Stern and his wife, Michelle.

Drinks and dinner were served at the table beginning at 7:00 p.m. All of the guests arrived on time. They ate a salad and a surf-and-turf combo of a small filet of beef and a lobster tail. For dessert, Ruth had the chef prepare a flaming baked Alaska, which drew oohs and aahs from the guests.

Conversation mainly centered around introductions and discussions of each other's specific vocations.

Finally, over coffee, Ham tapped on his water glass to get everyone's attention.

"Folks, I want to thank you all for coming tonight. I wanted to express my thanks and appreciation to all of you who have helped me in this latest adventure of mine. It has taken us from the beautiful south course of the Split Rock Golf Club into jail and out again, to a fracking site, to the house of a Mafia banker, and finally back here for this grand dinner.

"I want to express my thanks to Ben and Al, who got me out of jail and restored me to the loving bosom of ARNI and the Split Rock board and staff."

Everyone laughed at the reference to ARNI.

"I have even been made marshal at the Club's championship tournament tomorrow." Everyone applauded.

"I especially want to thank FBI Agent Linda Carter, who got my … behind … out of trouble more times than I can count. And Dr. Jane Bromly, who brought pure, clean water back to the Split Rock Golf Club and plans to keep it that way.

"I also want to thank my wonderful wife, Ruth, who has stuck with me, lovingly, no matter how much trouble I've gotten into. We are all happy and safe and sound here tonight, but we still haven't completely solved the original mystery of what, or who, killed Martin Rasher. So I thought I'd give each of you with some knowledge of the subject a chance to fill us in on what you know; then we all can go home and not worry any longer about the tale of death on the golf course. Linda, why don't you start."

"Thanks, Ham. Let's start with the golf partners, Al Ducasian, and Ben Fowler. Al's only crime was an acute case of paranoia over his fracking site being the source of the contaminant in the water that Marty Rasher swallowed, and that contaminant being responsible for his death. There is no proof that the fracking site was responsible for Martin Rasher's death.

"On the other hand, he was responsible for ultimately siring his grandchildren, and for allowing them to use his vehicle to mount an attack, categorized as attempted murder, against myself and Dr. Bromly and Dr. Marks, which resulted in a federal fine of $50,000. That gets the grandchildren out of trouble as well, as long as they don't own a firearm, don't drive a vehicle for three years, and spend one hundred hours each performing community service.

"Ben Fowler's story is different. The Federal BOLO, or 'be on the lookout' posting, resulted in his being located in a rented hunting lodge in the Poconos. He was returned to Philadelphia by a federal marshal. He was indicted by a grand jury for attempted murder, based on the evidence that Ham and I found. By the way, his thumbprint and DNA were found on the tack head discovered in Marty Rasher's shoe. Also, his name and address were identified on the invoice from the Birds and Bees

Company for the bee venom that was identified by a federal laboratory on the tip of the tack in Mr. Rasher's shoe. He was freed on a bond of $250,000. His trial is expected within six months, during which time he has been relieved of his passport. Prosecutors I have spoken to have told me that the evidence against him should result in a finding of guilty, a loss of his law license, and incarceration for between five and ten years. And there is no chance that he will be allowed to collect his residual legal fee from the estate of Martin Rasher.

"Mrs. Millie Rasher has been found not guilty of anything but silliness. She will have to testify in the federal case against Vincent 'Vinnie' DeLucca, but until the case is brought, she will have to continue to pay for the mortgage loan. She may be entitled to a finder's fee for turning in the banker, but not until she squares things away with the treasury department for taxes on all the donut money that she and Marty hid in the barbecue pit. I'm afraid her legal and accounting fees are going to eat considerably into her retirement fund.

"Okay, who's left? Oh, Vinnie. Yes, Vinnie will definitely end up in a federal prison for his activities as a nonbank banker, but he will be joined by many of his good fellows by the time the FBI completes its case.

"But there's a direct connection between Vinnie and Martin Rasher's demise. You see, one of the reasons Marty enjoyed Vinnie's cannoli so much and could never reproduce the slightly bitter taste of the delicacy was the fact that Vinnie added a pinch of strychnine to the cannoli. Strychnine is used as a rat killer, and Vinnie's house apparently had several of those creatures around that he used strychnine on. We know that because some neighbors of Vinnie's, in beautiful Montclair, New Jersey, complained that he was putting out some substance that sickened and, in one case, killed their dogs. The police were called in and found the bottle of strychnine in his garage. As far as the cannoli are concerned, I had two of them that Ham and I brought back from Millie Rasher's house analyzed at a federal lab. They both tested positive for strychnine. There was not enough in any single cannoli to kill a human being.

"The autopsy finding in the toxicology report, from Marty Rasher, did show minute amounts of strychnine in the blood plasma. Again, not a fatal level. But on rechecking samples of Marty's kidney and liver tissue, there was a clearly discernible level of strychnine. Therefore, while strychnine was not the single cause of Marty Rasher's death, it was a precipitating factor, along with other factors that served to weaken Marty's ability to fight back against other causes of death.

"Since the application of strychnine in an illegal payback scheme would hold up as one of the violent methods utilized by the Mafia for payback, it will be become a part of the circumstantial case against Vincent DeLucca. And that's about all I have to say."

"Well, that's plenty," said Ham. "Thank you for all of your efforts. Dr. Bromly, do you have anything to add?"

"Well, Dr. Marks, while there was no evidence of any substantial leak from the fracking sites on Mr. Ducasian's land, there was a fine levied by the Pennsylvania Department of Environmental Protection of $10,000 for the leak that occurred while Linda, Dr. Marks, and I were onsite.

"Investigation as to the cause of this leak showed no one single person to be involved. The hose clamp on that pressured tank of brine failed. The clamp was manufactured in China. All similar clamps have been removed and replaced throughout Pennsylvania by clamps produced by another manufacturer. The incident has been reported nationally, and the federal EPA will check on clamp replacement across the country.

"The water serving the Split Rock Golf Club is safe and pure. This site will be an annual inspection site for the Pennsylvania DEP— including the closed water area on the former tenth tee of the south course. This inspection will occur at no cost to the club.

"The water analysis from the naturally contaminated water on the former tenth tee, showed a significantly elevated level of methane gas, plus certain heavy metals and benzene. Methane itself is colorless and odorless, but in combination with some of the other contaminants it can cause noxious odors and tastes.

"The amount of the contaminated water presumably swallowed by Martin Rasher should not have been enough to cause his death. However, he might have been allergic to one or more of the contaminants, which in the face of the other physiologically damaging agents that we know about in this case certainly could have contributed to his demise."

"Well, thank you Dr. Bromly, for your expertise and your solution to a potentially serious problem here at Split Rock. I'm sure I speak for the board when I express our sincere appreciation. Al or Ben, do you have anything to add?"

Ben spoke up. "Ham, as long as you and Ruth are now safe from any prosecution in the matter, and as far as I am concerned you are, I am a happy man."

Al Stern, the criminal defense attorney, then said, "Ham, your record is clear in the matter of the death of Martin Rasher. In fact, someone ought to give you a Good Samaritan Medal."

"Well, maybe that's what the tournament marshal's hat is all about," Ham said. "Thank you all so very much. While we haven't honed in on one thing that killed Martin Rasher, we sure have presented a number of contributing factors and have seen to the mapping out of punishment to all of the bad guys in the story. I hope you have all enjoyed your dinner, and I hope to see you all on even happier occasions in the future."

And with that, the party broke up with handshakes and smiles, and some trading of personal cards.

Chapter Twenty-Four

MARSHAL MARKS

The designated marshal of a major golf tournament has certain assigned responsibilities. He or she sees that the proper players start at the 1ˢᵗ tee at their properly assigned starting times. The marshal sees to it that play is carried out at the proper speed, so as not to inconvenience any of the later-starting players. The marshal sees to it that players stick to the rules of play, both those in the USGA rule book and those that pertain to the local course. Golf disputes concerning play may be handled by the marshal or may be referred to the golf committee for the tournament. The marshal starts and stops the tournament under the direction of the committee.

Alternatively, the tournament marshal plays purely a ceremonial role. In that case, the marshal is expected to drive his or her golf cart around the tournament, dressed in the ceremonial clothes or wearing the ceremonial badge, and smile and wave to everybody he or she sees on the course.

"Don't forget to smile and wave at everyone, Ham," Ruth instructed as she sat in the golf cart that was carrying the waving pennant of the marshal of the Split Rock Golf Club Championship Tournament on this beautiful first Saturday in October.

"I won't, dear," Ham said with a smile. He was in his golf clothes, with tan slacks, a golf shirt with the logo of the Split Rock Golf Club on it, and wearing a golf hat with the golf logo overprinted with the word "Marshal" in white letters.

"Do you have the list of players and their starting times?" Ruth asked.

"I do. It's right on the clipboard attached to the windshield," Ham answered.

"And the USGA rule book?" Ruth continued.

"Yes. It's right here in my shirt pocket," Ham answered, maintaining his crowd-pleasing smile.

"Then I think we're all set to go to the first tee. It's a good idea for the marshal to be there early. I'm so proud of you, Ham," Ruth said.

"Well, thank you, dear. Before we start, I want to tell you my favorite golf joke."

"Golf joke? You memorized a golf joke?" Ruth said with an element of surprise.

"Well, it's my favorite," Ham stated.

"Well, go ahead, dear. I'm all ears," Ruth said, glancing at her watch and then relaxing in the cart seat when she saw that they had plenty of time to get to the first tee of the north course.

"It goes like this," Ham began, temporarily dropping his fixed smile. "Three men are finishing their round of golf on the eighteenth green. One of the men's wives comes walking onto the green. She approaches her husband and asks, 'John, dear, didn't you start out as a foursome? What has happened to the fourth man?'

"'Oh, my dear, it was awful. Bob Jones dropped dead on the tenth tee.'

"'Oh that's just terrible news,' his wife said.

"'It sure was,' said her husband. 'It was just hit and drag, hit and drag, hit and drag, for nine holes!'" Ham ended the joke with a chuckle.

Ruth didn't say a word for a moment. Then she grimaced, smiled, and said, "That's a terrible joke, Ham. But I can see where it strikes some golf-mannered humor."

"Yes," said Ham. "Golf-mannered humor indeed." Then he broke into a smile, waved to a passing golf player, and drove the golf cart, with its pennant flying, off to the first tee.

END

Printed in the United States
By Bookmasters